"So tell me what you believe my type is," Wade persisted.

"I've heard what people say about you, and in this case I believe they're right."

The left corner of his mouth lifted slightly. "You listen to rumors?"

"Sometimes. When it might affect my son."

He nodded, almost as if he approved her decision. "And rumor says...?"

"You have two criteria." Geneva held up one finger. "Female..." Then a second. "And breathing."

Taking her hand in his he unfolded her third finger. "Don't forget 'beautiful.'"

He gripped her with a gaze so intense that Geneva became lost in the forest-green depths of his eyes.

He cleared his throat and cast her a wolfish grin. "Guess that makes you my type after all."

Dear Reader,

As senior editor for the Silhouette Romance line, I'm lucky enough to get first peek at the stories we offer you each month. Each editor searches for stories with an emotional impact, that make us laugh or cry or feel tenderness and hope for a loving future. And we do this with *you*, the reader, in mind. We hope you continue to enjoy the variety each month as we take you from first love to forever....

Susan Meier's wonderful story of a hardworking single mom and the man who sweeps her off her feet is *Cinderella and the CEO*. In *The Boss's Baby Mistake*, Raye Morgan tells of a heroine who accidentally gets inseminated with her new boss's child! The fantasy stays alive with Carol Grace's *Fit for a Sheik* as a wedding planner's new client is more than she bargained for....

Valerie Parv always creates a strong alpha hero. In *Booties and the Beast*, Sam's the strong yet tender man. Julianna Morris's lighthearted yet emotional story *Meeting Megan Again* reunites two people who only *seem* mismatched. And finally Carolyn Greene's *An Eligible Bachelor* has a very special secondary character—along with a delightful hero and heroine!

Next month, look for our newest ROYALLY WED series with Stella Bagwell's *The Expectant Princess*. Marie Ferrarella astounds readers with *Rough Around the Edges*—her 100th title for Silhouette Books! And, of course, there will be more stories throughout the year chosen just for you.

Happy reading!

Mary-Theresa Hussey

Mary-Theresa Hussey
Senior Editor

Please address questions and book requests to:
Silhouette Reader Service
U.S.: 3010 Walden Ave., P.O. Box 1325, Buffalo, NY 14269
Canadian: P.O. Box 609, Fort Erie, Ont. L2A 5X3

An Eligible Bachelor

CAROLYN GREENE

SILHOUETTE *Romance*®

Published by Silhouette Books

America's Publisher of Contemporary Romance

This book is dedicated to Sean Eastwood,
who has taught a lot of people about the power of love.

And to Charles and William Hine who inspire me.

Also, many thanks to Byron Foutch for sharing
his knowledge of birds and their nesting habits.

 SILHOUETTE BOOKS

ISBN 0-373-19503-6

AN ELIGIBLE BACHELOR

Copyright © 2001 by Carolyn Greene

Visit Silhouette at www.eHarlequin.com

Printed in U.S.A.

CAROLYN GREENE

has been married to a fire chief for more than twenty years. She laughingly introduces herself as the one who lights the fires and her husband as the one who puts them out. They are a true opposites-attract type of couple and, because of this, they and their two teenagers have learned a lot about the art of compromise.

Coming together...mentally, physically and spiritually. That's what romance is all about, and that's what Carolyn strives to portray in her highly entertaining novels. Says Carolyn, "I like to think that after someone has read one of my books, I've made her or his day a little brighter. You just can't put a price tag on that kind of job satisfaction."

Dear Reader,

Fifteen years ago, a baby boy with a big personality came into my next-door neighbors' lives. Doctors diagnosed him with a rare genetic disorder, Joubert Syndrome, and predicted that little Sean would never sit up, talk or even smile.

Although it's known that Joubert Syndrome is genetically transmitted by both parents, testing is not currently available to determine whether they are carriers. Typical features of Joubert Syndrome, caused by a malformed or missing part of the brain (cerebellar vermis), include alternating episodes of panting and non-breathing in babies, poor balance and coordination, abnormal eye and tongue movements and decreased muscle tone. In addition, there are developmental delays and some degree of mental retardation is common. Since this is such a rare condition, it often goes undiagnosed or is misdiagnosed as Dandy Walker Syndrome or Cerebral Palsy.

Fortunately, Sean was too young to understand the doctor's grim prognosis. Today, he sits in his wheelchair, communicates through sign language and wears an ever-present smile. His mother served on the first Board of Directors for the Joubert Foundation, and the family has met others from all over the world with children like Sean and subsequently shared their experiences and struggles with me.

For more information about Joubert Syndrome, go to the Web site at http://www.joubertfoundation.com, or send a self-addressed stamped envelope care of Mary Van Damme, Joubert Syndrome Foundation, 12348 Summer Meadow Road, Rock, MI 49880.

All the best,

Carolyn Greene

Chapter One

The first thing Wade noticed was a red shoe, sitting like a misplaced rhododendron blossom among the clusters of blue hydrangea balls. And beside it a denim skirt and two shapely female legs protruding from the window. One foot sported a shoe that matched the one in the bush.

Not bothering to suppress a grin, Wade grabbed the shoe from the stalky branches and closed the distance between them. The woman's little boy threw him a shy smile and moved back to watch.

Geneva wriggled, trying to squeeze her way inside with sheer willpower, but the bottom edge of the pull-down window bit into the small of her back, forcing her to give up the battle she'd been fighting for several minutes. This was all because of a couple of birds who were more successful in their life plans than she had been.

A light May breeze swept past, teasing the hem of

her denim skirt and grazing her bare calves. If she pulled her knees close to the house and pointed her toes, she could touch an espadrille to the wooden planks of the small patio deck flanking her apartment at the back of her landlord's old Victorian house.

Her toddler son poked her rump with his tiny finger. "Funny mama."

Funny, indeed!

The embarrassment of being found like this—after only one day in her new place—was of less concern than the humiliation she would feel at having failed to live up to the agreement she'd struck with her landlord. Sean, her landlord's nineteen-year-old disabled brother who occupied the apartment adjacent to hers, might be able to give her a hand. But one of the terms of her lease was that she'd be available to help Sean when needed. If she had to seek help from the young man she was supposed to watch out for, Wade Matteo would be justified in doubting her ability to perform the simple job. Worse, he might revoke the lease she'd recently signed.

And if she lost this apartment—with its reasonable rent and beautiful surroundings—she'd be forced to move back to the city. Then her chance of saving for a down payment on a house would disappear. And along with it, her dream of giving her son the roots she'd always longed for would vanish.

Jacob fidgeted behind her and proceeded to dance an awkward jig. "Gotta go potty."

Of course. When it rained, it poured…so to speak.

His agenda for the afternoon—go through his black book, call some of the women who met his criteria and try to sweet-talk them into giving him what he wanted—would have to wait.

When he had returned home a few moments ago and pointed the nose of his elegant black sports car toward the garage at the left side of his house, he had heard a woman's voice. Considering his new tenant's domestic tendencies, Wade had assumed she was singing as she did her housework. During the past week, the lovely Ms. Jensen had been cleaning and gradually moving her belongings into the apartment.

Not that he was surprised. The first time he'd met her to show her the apartment, he'd immediately pegged her as a young June Cleaver. The single mother didn't have the high-heeled shoes or strand of pearls, or even a husband, as the old-fashioned TV character had, but he knew with certainty she had the nesting instinct. And that spelled danger.

Long ago he'd learned to pick up on such clues, and less than a minute after he'd met his attractive tenant, he had mentally hung a Do Not Touch sign on her. And, as if to ward her off, a long-standing superstitious habit prompted him to rub the Bachelor of the Year pin on his collar. Women who sang while they did housework were definitely off his list of possibilities.

He crossed the driveway to the deck behind the attached apartment. Amusing as this might be, he'd have to make this quick. His little black book held promise for a fruitful evening.

"Sean?" Her cry was plaintive now, as if she'd given up hope that anyone would come to her rescue.

Odd that she would be calling his brother for help. The Joubert syndrome that weakened Sean's muscles forced him to walk with crutches and prevented him from lifting heavy objects. It was Saturday afternoon, so the teen was no doubt driving his cart around the course as he picked up trash, retrieved lost golf balls and chatted with the country-club guests.

Geneva stiffened as if she must have felt the vibrations when he crossed the wood-planked patio.

From her facedown position, she pushed a hand out the window and motioned him closer. "I thought you'd never get me out of this mess. Do me a favor, and don't mention this to your brother, okay?"

"And why wouldn't you want him to know?"

"Mr. Matteo?"

"You can call me Wade." Out of habit, he fell into his come-a'calling voice…a deep, rich tone that he'd cultivated to go along with his playboy persona.

She wiggled her toes, and he knew instinctively that he'd gotten to her. "Would you please lift this window off my back?"

Geneva tried to keep the panic out of her voice. Like it or not, she was at his mercy.

"How do I know you're not a burglar? Maybe I should call the sheriff."

"Come on, you rented the place to me just last week. You know who I am."

"Now that you mention it, I do recognize the legs."

Geneva automatically tugged at her skirt to make sure she wasn't showing him more than just lack of coordination with the window.

Her ex-husband, Les, would have a field day with her predicament if he were here. Fortunately, he and his relentless put-downs were long gone now. She only hoped her landlord had more restraint.

Geneva grew warm when she remembered the first

time she'd seen Wade. With looks like his, it was easy to understand why women practically stood in line to go out with him, and she had responded to his blatantly masculine charm by blushing and succumbing to a fit of shyness. Once again he was making her feel inexperienced and naive…which, come to think of it, she was.

Strong male hands gripped the small of her back, and Geneva stiffened at their touch.

"Bear with me a moment," he said, his arm nudging her bottom as he braced his elbows on either side of her hips in an attempt to push the window up.

Although he'd started out teasing her, his actions were now matter-of-fact. Even so, she felt embarrassed at being caught with her rump up and her guard down. Geneva's abdomen chaffed against the frame, but there was little she could do with the window pressed firmly against her back. The thin scarlet T-shirt had worked its way loose from the waistband of her denim skirt and did little to cushion her from the wood biting into her body.

A moment later the window shuddered upward and Geneva was freed from its grasp. Backing gingerly out of its clutches, she gathered her son close, then smoothed the tangle of brown curls that fell over her shoulders.

Momentarily forgetting to thank her rescuer, she lifted the hem of her top and inspected the damage. There was no blood from the scrape on her side, but a broad patch the size of her palm flamed a bright pink, and tiny ridges indicated where the skin had barely been broken.

Wade leaned close and made an appropriate noise of sympathy that somehow made her feel better.

"That's gotta hurt like he—" He interrupted himself, his gaze darting to Jacob. "—a lot."

Suddenly remembering she was exposing her midriff to a man who was not a doctor, Geneva jerked the fabric down without bothering to tuck it back into her skirt. She set about fussing with her clothes in an attempt to cover her awkwardness.

"You look great," he said in an obvious attempt to reassure her but, coming from him, the words served as a reminder to beware the reputed philanderer on her doorstep. He took her shoe from his hip pocket. "You dropped this, Cinderella."

Geneva reached to take it from him, but he had already knelt before her and cupped the heel of her bare foot in his hand.

"I feel like a regular Prince Charming," he announced as he slid the canvas shoe onto her foot.

Self-consciously, Geneva moved backward. The deck railing prevented further retreat.

"What? I don't bite."

She looked down at her feet and wondered why the heel he had cupped in his hand still burned from his touch. "That's not what the neighbors say."

She hadn't actually meant to say the words out loud, and she was all set to apologize, when he threw his head back and laughed. The deep sound of it wrapped around her, making her glad to have caused such a reaction, even if it had been accidental.

"Ah, so my reputation precedes me."

He didn't seem upset at having been the topic of discussion. Instead, he seemed amused by it. Perhaps he was used to such an occurrence.

"Let me put your fears to rest," he said, his gaze capturing hers with such an intensity that she couldn't have looked away if she had wanted to. "You're not my type."

With an involuntary squaring of her shoulders, she found herself annoyed rather than relieved by his declaration. There was nothing wrong with her. She was reasonably attractive, in pretty good shape, intelligent and, as a bonus, she was quite handy with most things domestic. And although her ex-husband had tried to make her believe otherwise, she was very easy to get along with.

At her skeptical "hmmph!" Wade raised an eyebrow. "Would you care to elaborate on that?"

"Not really." She lifted her chin, determined to set some ground rules. "Your personal life is none of my business, and I don't care what type of woman you prefer as long as you're discreet about it." She ruffled her son's hair. "It wouldn't do to have a certain someone asking questions about the birds and bees because of our neighbor's activities."

Besides, she'd already shared a roof with one skirt chaser. She had no desire to repeat the experience.

"You think you have me pegged."

She took Jacob's hand and started toward the house, but he intercepted her. Her gaze fell squarely on the broad wall of his chest, which blocked her view but presented her with an even better one.

"So tell me what you believe my type is," he persisted.

Geneva crossed her arms in front of her and immediately regretted the action when it caused the shirt to rub her sore spot. "I've heard what people say about you, and in this case I believe they're right."

The left corner of his mouth lifted slightly. "You listen to rumors?"

She looked down, pausing a moment to send Jacob to ride on his tricycle. When he was engaged in his play, she admitted to Wade, "Sometimes. When it might affect my son."

Such as when she'd heard whisperings that Les was seeing another woman during his supposed business trips. She hadn't stuck her head in the sand then, and she wasn't about to start with Wade Matteo.

He nodded, almost as if he approved her decision. "And rumor says…"

He was not going to let up until she told him, so she may as well deliver it with both barrels. "You have two criteria." She held up one finger. "Female…" Then a second. "…and breathing."

Taking her hand in his, he unfolded her third finger. "Don't forget 'beautiful.'"

Then, failing to release her hand, he gripped her with a gaze so intense that Geneva became lost in the forest-green depths of his eyes. Right now she felt less like Cinderella, whom he'd mentioned earlier, and more like Little Red Riding Hood. *What big, dark eyes he had.*

He cleared his throat and cast her a wolfish grin. "Guess that makes you my type after all."

Geneva blinked. This was getting out of hand. Pulling away from his touch, she sought to escape into the relative safety of her new home.

"Thank you for helping me out of my predicament." She withdrew her fingers from his grasp as casually as if they'd been shaking hands and sidestepped him to go back to the window. Flashing him a grateful smile, she added, "Next time I'll find a stick to prop the window open while I'm climbing through."

Wade moved toward her. His expression was no longer hungry, but filled with concern. "Next time you lock yourself out, just ask me for the spare key. There's no need to risk getting hurt."

"Oh, I didn't lock myself out." She wondered if, like her ex-husband, Wade would laugh at her sentimentality. Letting go of the window, she knew she couldn't go through life reacting to her ex and his hang-ups. Just because Les didn't share her love for babies didn't mean all men were like that. And just because this particular man—crisp slacks, muscle-hugging shirt and raw masculinity—seemed less like a family man than any she'd ever met before, that didn't mean he wouldn't understand her softhearted reason for finding an alternate entry into the house, no matter how inconvenient it might be.

Nodding toward the decorative summer wreath on her one and only outside door, she gave him the short version. "A couple of squatters have moved in without paying rent."

With a frown of dawning comprehension, Wade crossed to the mat in front of the door.

Standing on the ornate braided script that spelled out Welcome, he considered the irony. For him, her body language had spelled out Go Away. Not that he could blame her. Although he'd joked about her not being his type, it was clear they both saw danger signals in the other.

Lifting his gaze to the grapevine wreath she'd placed there a couple of days after signing the lease, Wade felt her presence as she came up behind him. He inhaled her scent and tried to place the wholesome aroma that tugged at his memory. As ridiculous as it seemed, he could have sworn she smelled like fresh-baked cookies. Or maybe cinnamon strudel.

Letting out a large breath, Wade reminded himself to stay focused on the matter at hand. He needed to get her inside—and quickly—so he could put a safe distance between them.

"See?" She brushed his arm as she pointed to the bottom curve of the wreath. "It's inside that clump of brown grass."

He had to look close to see the grass that had been added after she'd hung it. It was hidden behind an ornamental bird covered in blue-dyed feathers, and the dried strands camouflaged well within the door decoration.

Leaning in, he got a glimpse of a black-crowned head and an unblinking eye fixed on him. Their gazes held for a split second before the panicked bird darted from the creative nest, its flapping gray wings whirring so close that the breeze hit Wade's face.

Dodging to avoid a collision, he bumped into Geneva, who had been hovering near his elbow.

"I told you," she said as if he'd doubted her word. "Now look inside the nest."

Wade hesitated, wondering what further surprises lurked within the otherwise ordinary-looking wreath. Curiosity soon got the best of him, and he chanced another approach to peer inside.

This time he was rewarded with a glimpse of a small speckled white egg tucked away in the down-lined nest.

Geneva leaned toward him, her head almost touching his as they examined the fragile contents. Wade inhaled again. The scent of her, a light vanilla fragrance mixed with something else, made him hungry. And not for food.

"I noticed it this morning. After last night's rain, the door was sticking as I tried to close it. So I gave it a firm tug and a bird flew out, like it did just now." Reaching forward, she secured a stray bit of grass behind the fake bird that served double duty as sentinel and nest anchor. "It's a wonder the egg didn't fall out."

And a good thing, too, or his maudlin new tenant would have been wracked with remorse and self-blame. "A bird that looks like yours makes its nest in the eaves of the clubhouse porch every year. Our golf pro says it's a tufted titmouse. There will be four or five eggs in there by the end of the week. You're going to have company for another month or so until the babies fly away."

Geneva's reaction to that bit of news was to grab a loose tendril of hair that had escaped from the clip at the nape of her neck and twist it around her finger. No fancy manicure for her. Her fingernails had been filed to a serviceable length and covered with a clear gloss. Feminine yet unpretentious, just like Geneva.

Wade thought of the woman he'd been with last night. Her nails had been overlaid with acrylic tips of unrealistic proportions, painted a bright magenta, and each imbedded with a tiny diamond-like chip. He doubted they would survive normal day-to-day working conditions, not that they had to. The important thing was that they hadn't hampered her ability to fulfill his need.

By now, Jacob had bored of circling his tricycle around the dogwood tree beside the deck. The little boy whose cinnamon-brown eyes and light olive skin matched his mother's, clutched the front of his pale green shorts. Toddling to Geneva, he tugged her skirt and gave her a pleaded *Mommy!''*

She stooped and picked him up. "Oh, I'm sorry, honey. I forgot all about your problem." Her eyes met Wade's, making it clear he was the reason for her distraction. The gesture reminded him that it would be better for both of them to handle this situation with expediency.

She was heading back to the window, the boy in her arms. Although Kinnon Falls was a small town populated by law-abiding folks whose main concern was raising their families in a slow-paced, peaceful environment, he didn't like the idea of his new tenant entering and leaving through an unlocked window. A nestful of birds wasn't worth the risk.

"No, wait," he said, stopping her with a hand to her arm.

Her skin, smooth and warm, enticed him to explore further. To move in a gentle caress up over her shoulder and trail across her collarbone to the beckoning hollow at the base of her throat. Her eyes shuttered as if his touch had sent her to a similar place of longing. He knew the look, knew that she was a woman who was passionate about life and who could be equally passionate in bed. But she was also passionate about a lifestyle he wanted to avoid.

He withdrew his hand from her arm. "You can go in through the connecting door inside my house."

The delicate wings of her eyebrows drew together, causing a narrow crease above her small nose. He knew without asking that she was considering his reputation.

"Just for now," he assured her. "Until we can figure out another solution." He would have offered her a key to his house but, considering her wariness toward him, he thought it best to wait on that.

Geneva gave him a reluctant nod and taking Jacob's hand, they followed him in through the garage. As they went, he explained that the two apartments had been added by his parents when he was a teen. "Your place was occupied by my grandmother after she'd broken her hip. That way, she could live independently, but it was close enough to allow my parents and me to check on her every day."

Just as Geneva was now doing for his younger brother.

"Was Sean's apartment originally for your other set of grandparents?" she asked.

He grinned as he entered the den and unlatched the connecting door between their residences. "It was for me. When I was seventeen, I had such an active life, with people coming and going all the time that it was distracting to the rest of the family. So when they built the apartment for Nana, they had the contractor do one for me as well."

Geneva could feel her eyes grow large at his revelation, and she tried to squelch her reaction. It wouldn't do to have her eyes pop out, right here in her landlord's house. Even so, it was a shock to discover that his proclivities had started at such a young age...and that his parents had condoned it.

In an article in the local newspaper last year, he'd been named the town's Most Eligible Bachelor. The author of the article had used words such as *playboy* and *rake* to describe him.

And then it had referenced another equally dubious distinction in which the mayor had proclaimed her landlord Bachelor of the Year and presented him with a gold pin. Geneva wondered if that was the same pin he wore on his collar and touched frequently as if it was some sort of lucky charm.

This information she'd regrettably discovered only *after* she'd signed the lease. If she'd known of his social standing beforehand, she wouldn't currently be worrying that someone might have seen her enter his house. In fact, she'd be living somewhere else altogether.

One thing was for certain. If she had gone elsewhere, her surroundings wouldn't be nearly as beautiful, nor would the place be as affordable. And she doubted she'd be able to save for a house of her own…a dream Les had trampled before their divorce.

As it was now, her modest apartment, located smack in the center of Kinnon Falls's most exclusive residential community, overlooked a postcard-beautiful lake with a lush green golf course beyond it. To the left, about a ten-minute walk away, the country club and gardens created the perfect setting for outdoor parties and receptions. So far, she and Jacob had seen two such parties, their Japanese lanterns twinkling beneath a star-studded sky.

Releasing the latch on the door connecting their living quarters, Wade gave a push, but something on the other side refused to give. Casting a knowing glance at her, he stated rather than asked, "You added another lock, didn't you?"

Of course she did! As the owner of the Country Club he might be the most successful businessman in Kinnon Falls, and he might have his pick of any of the area's most influential society women, but she wasn't taking any chances. Not that he'd be interested. Even so, she had her own reputation to consider.

"Gotta *go!*" Jacob reminded her with renewed urgency.

"It'll take me a few minutes to climb through your window and unlock your new security hardware." He pointed past her. "You can take him down the hall to the first door on the right."

As she took her son through the house, she noted with relief that the portion of the dwelling she saw seemed very ordinary. Nothing gave testimony to the wild life her landlord was reputed to lead. No beaded curtains, overly large mirrors, mood music or other evidence that this place might serve as a seduction palace. The decor was masculine and free of frills but tastefully elegant with its heavy rosewood furniture and Oriental rugs. And, for a bachelor's place, the area was surprisingly neat. The only thing that stood out to her was the pinball machine that commanded one corner of the den.

They returned a few minutes later to find Wade standing beside the open door. The amusement in his green eyes told her what he'd found even before he spoke the words.

"You added a slide lock *and* a chain?"

She squirmed under his perusal, anxious to get back to the sanctuary of her apartment and put the closed door and three locks between them. "One can never be too careful these days."

"So true," he said as if confirming that she had reason to be wary of him. Well, at least he didn't pretend to be something he was not. "Which brings me to the problem of your getting in and out of your place."

Reaching into a cut-glass dish on the coffee table, he withdrew a couple of chocolate candies, handed one to Jacob, and offered the other to her. When she refused, he gave that one to Jacob as well. Her son smiled and promptly expressed his thanks by sitting on his benefactor's Italian-leather loafer while he removed the paper. Geneva started to say they hadn't had dinner yet, then decided to let it slide this time. With any luck, they wouldn't have much contact with each other after this.

"My golf pro knows a lot about birds. I'll check with him to see if we can safely move the nest to a more convenient location." He reached into his hip pocket, pulled out a wallet with a familiar designer logo and retrieved a key from it. "In the meantime, you can use my spare key for access to your place."

Geneva took a step back, holding her hands up, palms facing outward. "No, I don't think that will be necessary." At the moment, she didn't have another solution, but she was hopeful that if she gave it enough thought she could come up with *something*.

His hand dropped to his side, fingers gripping the key tightly. "You're not afraid of me, are you?"

She was certain the offer was made out of generosity and concern for her and Jacob—at least, she hoped so. But she didn't want to offend him further than she already had by confessing her fear that his reputation might taint her own.

"You lead a busy life," she said at last. "I wouldn't want to interfere with your, uh, entertaining."

"You're in luck," he said, pushing the key toward her once again. "I only hold my orgies every other month. This is my month to rest up and study the videos.''

Before she could stop herself from reacting to his outrageous statement, Geneva felt her mouth drop open. Recovering as well as she could, she said, partly to assure herself, ''You're just teasing me.'' Even so, she felt it necessary to refuse the proffered key. When he didn't crack a smile, she added, ''Aren't you?''

Wade frowned. He couldn't blame her for believing the things she'd heard about him…hell, he'd intentionally started some of those rumors himself.

With other women, he felt relief upon seeing their expressions of wary unease. His dubious reputation helped keep them at a safe emotional distance. When they accompanied him to galas, social functions and charity benefits, they did so with the full knowledge that he was a for-the-moment kind of man. They made no demands on him and held no expectations beyond the evening's events. If he was lucky—and he often was—he managed to get them to share their carefully guarded assets. And when they did, they gave willingly, expecting nothing in return. And he liked it like that.

But that same wariness clouding Geneva's normally bright, open features seemed out of place on her. Something told him it was a maternal reaction…a reaction borne of concern for her son more than for herself.

For the first time in many years he found himself wanting to shatter the illusion he'd so carefully crafted. But he couldn't do that, couldn't expose his true self, especially not to a home-and-hearth kind of woman like Geneva. The stakes were too high for him to let her see the person he kept hidden away from public scrutiny. If he let down his guard, he might find himself wanting what he'd been denying himself ever since...

Wade gritted his teeth. There was no use mulling over the past or the probability that it might be repeated for him in the future. But despite all this, he couldn't stop himself from proclaiming, "I'm not as bad as you think. I even go to church on a fairly regular basis."

The furrow between her eyebrows disappeared, and a broad smile spread across her face, forming dimpled brackets on either side of her mouth. "Really? I've been looking for one in this area. Jacob and I would love to go to your church on Sunday." She removed a rumpled tissue from her skirt pocket, wiped the chocolate from her son's hands and drew him toward the door Wade had unlocked earlier. "Perhaps you could introduce us to some of your friends."

Wade felt like a bobcat treed by a Chihuahua. Feeling cornered and scared, and a little foolish that such a tiny woman could elicit these emotions in him, he contemplated all the trouble that had arisen since she'd moved in. First, she'd sent his libido into overdrive despite the fact that she embodied every quality he tried to avoid in a woman. Then, thanks to her door wreath that spelled out an open invitation to a pair of family-minded birds, she had cost him his privacy. And now she was working her way into his personal life. He'd better do something about this latest development, and somehow put her out of his reach, before his heart and hormones overruled his head.

Propelling Jacob into her apartment with a light pat to the boy's bottom, she flashed Wade a warm, open smile that nearly undid years of carefully constructed armor. "I'll see you at church."

And that was when Wade knew what he would have to do.

Chapter Two

Geneva hoped to take Jacob to the toddler-age Sunday-school class without either of them crying. He'd had a lot of changes in his young life, first losing a father—bum that he was—and then moving to a whole new community. There were some positive changes, too, such as the wide-open yard for him to play in and a new friendship with Sean, who doted on the boy and took him for rides on his golf cart. But the changes, both good and bad, were creating stress, and her son had become slightly clingy in the past few weeks.

His reaction had made her more resolved than ever to find just the right house for Jacob to grow up in. The only child of a military man, Geneva had gone through more than her share of uprootings, and she wanted to give her son the kind of stable home environment she had longed for as a child...and still wanted.

And while she was dreaming, her idea of the per-

fect upbringing for her son included a strong and loving father and a handful of siblings. She'd gone into
her relationship with Les harboring this same dream
for their future. Although she'd seen evidence of his
party-boy ways, she had believed him when he'd told
her that her happiness was his foremost concern.
She'd thought he would settle into family life after
Jacob was born, but he soon found more excuses to
be away from the house. Away from her and his child.

"You really didn't need to drive us to church,"
she said as Wade pulled his car into the parking lot.
"We could have met you here." All weekend long,
she'd had to impose on him to answer the door each
time they'd needed to enter or exit the apartment
through his house. And on the one occasion they both
had to go out, he'd hidden a key in the hanging basket
of begonias that adorned the broad front porch. It was
a hassle doing it this way, no doubt about it, but she
had no desire to encourage any more togetherness
than was absolutely necessary.

"It's no bother. Because of the rain, I doubt we'll
have any but the most diehard golfers at the course
this morning." He looked at her strangely, as if something was on his mind, but he only sighed and added,
"Sometimes I have to miss church, especially when
it's sunny and mild, but now that you know the
way..."

Then she understood. He was saying, in essence,
after this you're on your own. He was doing the hos-
pitable thing today, bringing her here and introducing
her around, but he was making it clear this was not
to become a habit. Well, that was perfectly okay with
her.

Once inside, Sean and Jacob walked ahead as

Wade led Geneva past the adult classes, the high-school class, and eventually stopped at the fifth-grade room.

"I want to get Jacob to the nursery." Her gaze remained fixed on Sean, who was making faces at her laughing son as they waited for her and Wade to catch up.

Wade straightened his tie before answering. "There's someone I want you to meet first. Sean, why don't you take Jacob to the nursery for Geneva?"

Her protective instincts kicked in as she imagined her son feeling helpless and abandoned in a new place. "But I was going to take him."

Oblivious to her concern, Jacob grasped the older fellow's coattail and left without a backward glance. She supposed she should have been glad he went along so easily, carefully dodging Sean's crutches, but instead she felt as though she'd been forgotten in the excitement of the moment.

"He'll probably cry," she protested. And if he did, who would hold him and comfort him until his tears dried?

"It's better this way," Wade assured her. "Kids are less likely to cry when they leave Mom than when Mom leaves them. You can check on him through the two-way mirror when we're done here."

"Since when did you get to be an authority on children?" she muttered. She hadn't intended for him to hear her grousing, but the upward quirk of his mouth told her he'd caught it all.

"Since I helped raise my younger brother," he replied.

Before she could respond, a dark-haired man in his

early thirties appeared at the classroom door. "May I help you?"

A roomful of eleven-year-olds studied them with keen interest.

"I'd like you to meet Geneva Jensen," Wade said without preamble. "She and her son are visiting our church for the first time today." Then, finishing the introduction, he pulled her by the elbow so that she was positioned squarely in front of the man. "Geneva, this is Deacon Tackett."

Geneva smiled shyly. If ever she'd felt put on the spot—on display, even—it was now. But she appreciated her landlord's friendly gesture, so she would just tough it out.

The gentleman before her seemed to sense her discomfort. After switching a bit of chalk to his left hand, he shook her hand and smiled warmly. It was a pleasant expression set against an attractive backdrop of dark eyebrows, aquiline nose and slim cheeks that carried what she suspected was an ever-present shadow of beard, and it went a long way toward making her feel welcome.

"It's so nice to meet you," he said. "I hope you'll like your visit enough to return and perhaps become a member of our congregation."

She was about to murmur a polite reply so they could excuse themselves gracefully, but Wade seemed determined to prolong the awkward conversation.

"The deacon teaches Sunday school to fifth-graders," he said, stating the obvious. "He really likes kids a lot…always organizing youth trips and having pizza parties for them."

"No need to be formal," the man said in response

to the manner in which Wade addressed him. "Please, call me Ellis." Ellis tilted his head as if suddenly realizing the implication behind the introduction. "Is your son in fifth grade? He's welcome to join our study class this morning."

"Oh, no, he's in the nursery." And she was getting antsy about checking to see how Jacob was accepting his new situation.

"Well, I'm glad Mr. Matteo stopped by to introduce us. If there's anything you need, or if you have any questions..."

That's when it hit her. These two men barely knew each other! Why else would they call each other Deacon Tackett and Mr. Matteo? Until now she had assumed Wade had merely wanted her to meet a friend of his. But they obviously weren't close, and she didn't have an older child for Ellis to teach, so why was Wade putting her through this?

"Geneva does a lot of sewing." Wade ignored Ellis's attempt to close the conversation and laid a hand on her shoulder. "Perhaps you could charm her into helping with the costumes for this year's Christmas play." The smile Wade flashed the other man seemed fraught with meaning. Then, turning to Geneva, he added, "The deacon is a real pillar of the community. His family has lived in the area for more than a century. They even have a road named after them."

Why was he telling her this? Not knowing how else to respond to this seemingly unnecessary bit of information, she merely said, "That's quite impressive."

Wade gave her an amused grin. "Personally, I'd rather have a roller coaster named after me."

She wasn't surprised. A date with Wade Matteo

was probably just like a roller-coaster ride—full of exciting turns, giddying heights and heart-stopping plummets, that ultimately ended up right where they started. Whoever dared to take such a ride would certainly have a story to tell and a memory to cherish, but nothing more.

Realization dawned with such crackling intensity that it nearly blinded her. Wade was setting her up, and he'd chosen to pair her with Ellis. She felt herself blush, not certain whether to get angry with him for being so presumptuous or go along with the matchmaking attempt.

Taking another, more assessing look at Ellis, she realized Wade had chosen wisely. Now, *there* was a man with whom she could go somewhere. From what little she knew about him—that he was a leader in the community, that he seemed kind and polite and, best of all, that he liked children—she decided this was someone she could possibly build a relationship with. There wouldn't be any hairpin turns or spiraling heights of ecstasy as in a roller-coaster ride perhaps, but he seemed like just the kind of man she and Jacob needed.

Ellis obviously hadn't caught on to Wade's machinations yet. He pointed at the two of them. "How long have you two been dating?"

"Oh, no, we're not dating," Geneva quickly supplied. "We just live together."

Wade gave her a look that told her she'd blown it, and then his Adam's apple bobbed as he tried to hold back a laugh.

"I mean we live in the same house." Suddenly the spring day seemed to have grown unseasonably warm, and Geneva realized she hadn't actually clarified the deacon's misconception after all. So she tried again. "I'm at the back, and he's in front."

Oh, good grief, that sounded even worse!

Ellis's blue eyes darkened as his gaze darted between them. Geneva had the sickening feeling that not only had she ruined her chances with him, but also with anyone who might talk to him.

To her relief, Wade fished her out of the hot water she'd gotten herself into.

"What she means is that I'm her landlord. Geneva lives in an apartment attached to the back of my house, which is next door to Sean."

Ellis's eyebrows descended to a more normal position, and he gave a soft chuckle. "Of course."

The conversation fell suddenly quiet, and Ellis glanced over his shoulder at the children who were swatting each other with their lesson books.

"Would you like to see it sometime?" Wade seemed impervious to her growing discomfort. "Tuesday evening, maybe?"

Geneva caught his elbow and gave it a squeeze. "I don't think—"

"Sure," said Ellis. By now the kids had stopped their horseplay and were chanting a jump-rope song about sitting in a tree and k-i-s-s-i-n-g. Ellis seemed not to hear as he smiled benevolently at Geneva. "Is seven o'clock okay?"

"That's perfect," Wade said, cutting off her protest. "Bring an appetite. I hear Geneva is quite the cook."

This was getting out of control. What would people think when they found out the town's resident playboy was procuring dates for her? What must Ellis think about this peculiar setup? A knot clutched at her stomach as she considered the expectations such an arrangement might arouse.

Wade stabbed at the buttons on the phone and stopped before he reached the last one. It should be such a simple thing to ask a wealthy heiress to accompany him to a charity ball, but he couldn't bring himself to punch that last number.

He felt like a phony...he didn't even like the woman. That had never stopped him before, so he couldn't understand why he was having so much trouble going through with it this time. Hell, he didn't even have this much trouble asking the deacon for a date with Geneva.

Maybe Geneva had something to do with his hesitation. He hadn't been the same since she moved in. At first he'd told himself it was because a single woman on the premises, especially one as wholesome and motherish as Geneva, tended to cramp his style. Instead, he found himself daydreaming about unfastening her hair clip and letting her rich brown locks tumble over his fingers. And if he wasn't careful, his thoughts led to imagining the softness of those curls tickling his bare chest as they lay together in each other's arms.

Then, to shake himself out of the foolhardy reverie, he reminded himself of his resolve to date only career women or those over forty who had no desire to add to their families. Geneva embodied every quality that he sought to avoid in women: she was in the prime of her childbearing years, making clear in actions and words her wish for a large family. She was the kind of woman who wanted permanence...and promises of things he could not fulfill.

Wade paced the kitchen floor, reminding himself that the end justified the means, and forced himself to redial the woman's number.

Cherise Watson was the daughter of a wealthy businessman-turned-senator, and though her father had died a few years ago, she and her mother still had strong ties to others in the political arena. Wade had long been a dedicated fundraiser for the children's hospital. Not only would a generous donation from Cherise provide the hospital with a new magnetic resonance imaging machine, but a well-placed word in the right politician's ear might garner the research funds the facility so desperately needed.

Geneva hoisted Jacob to her hip and allowed him to peek carefully into the nest at the two most recent additions. One of the parent birds sat in an oak tree, chirping its indignation at their intrusion. Setting her son down, she contemplated the best way to approach the problem. Although she thought her landlord could have been more subtle, and definitely more tactful, in his matchmaking effort, she was grateful that he had introduced her to such a nice man.

Fortunately, after church she was able to talk a bit more with Ellis without interruption from her busybody neighbor. Their conversation helped convince her that the deacon's desires mirrored her own. He loved children and wanted a traditional family life but, as was her own experience, his exacting standards narrowed the dating pool so that his options were severely limited.

She stood back from the house and examined the bare area beside the light fixture. If she moved the wreath those few feet, perhaps the parent birds would adapt without complaint to the minor adjustment. And she would regain the use of her door.

For the past couple of days, she'd been using Wade's house as a cut-through to her apartment. Despite his insistence that her entering and leaving through his living quarters was not an inconvenience, Geneva was equally insistent that she had to find another solution. Today. *Before* her upcoming dinner date with Ellis tomorrow night.

It was inconvenient to have Wade let her and Jacob through his house every time they needed to enter or exit. The situation could prove awkward if he had to serve as the gatekeeper for her date as well.

Considering the way in which Wade had meddled to bring her and Ellis together, she didn't want to give him an opportunity to meddle any more than he already had.

Mustering up his gumption, Wade took a deep breath and finished dialing the number. It was only for one evening, for crying out loud. And it was a public event, so it wasn't like he'd have to wine and dine Cherise privately...and risk giving her the impression that he harbored a romantic interest in her. The line on the other end rang once.

"Excuse me."

Startled, Wade wheeled around to find Geneva poised hesitantly on the threshold between his den and kitchen.

He sucked in his breath at the sight of her and dropped the phone back into its cradle. The trim white pants that ended in a slit just below her knees showed off a flat stomach, enticingly rounded hips and lightly tanned calves and ankles. As for the tailored blue shirt, it caressed her curves in a way his hands itched to mimic. And her hair, as usual, fought to escape the clip that held the riotous waves prisoner. A fragment of oak pollen clung near her temple, giving evidence that she'd been gardening or playing outside with Jacob. If she looked this good while just hanging around the house, he dared not imagine how easily she could outshine all the ladies who would be attending the hospital's charity ball later this month.

"I'm sorry to bother you, but I was wondering if I might borrow a hammer?"

Jacob crawled between her ankles. "Bam-bam-bam!" he said, imitating a popular Saturday-morning cartoon character.

"Sure, it's out in the utility room." He started to step past her and lead the way. But, preferring instead to savor this unexpected visual treat, he motioned for her to go ahead of him. The view from the back was as good as the front. His body reacted as if he'd just returned from spending several years in a monk's retreat. His overstimulated hormones had his nerve endings tingling with anticipation, and Wade knew if he didn't send her away immediately he might do or say something he'd regret later.

Grabbing three different sizes of hammers from his workstation, he shoved them all in her hands and abruptly turned and went back inside. Standing once again in front of the telephone, he tried to wipe the picture of her—eyes wide and lips puckered in an unspoken question—from his mind and return to the task he'd been avoiding for weeks.

Waiting a moment for his heart to stop racing, he once again forced himself to pick up the phone. But this time he couldn't bring himself to go through the motions of calling Cherise.

When Geneva returned a moment later, he felt rather than heard her enter the kitchen.

"I think I need a screwdriver after all."

"They're on the workbench where I got the hammers," he said, inviting her to help herself and save him the torture of having to refuse her round bottom's beckoning gesture as she exited the room.

Fortunately, she took his cue and left before a fit of conscience compelled him to change his mind.

Trying to pull his thoughts back to the matter at hand, Wade knew he couldn't wait any longer to find a date for the charity ball. Although there'd never been a shortage of willing ladies to accompany him to similar fund-raisers in the past, courtesy dictated that he give his guest ample time to book a fitting for a new dress and otherwise prepare for the event. With only two weeks to go, he was already pushing it to the wire.

Despite the urgency, he couldn't bring himself to focus on what he had to do. He was distracted, partly by the image of Geneva in those casual pants, and partly from wondering what she was up to with his tools. Remembering the shelves he'd promised to install over her sewing table, he wondered if she'd decided to put them up herself.

Happily abandoning his mission, he followed the path she'd taken through the garage to the back of the house.

Having anchored a screw in the wood siding beside her door, Geneva reached to lift the wreath from its current mooring.

"I wouldn't do that if I were you."

The deep male voice almost made her send the wreath—nest and all—crashing to the deck. "I wish you wouldn't sneak up on me!"

Ignoring the scolding tone in her words, Wade stated simply, "I talked to Tim, the golf pro, and he says the parents might abandon the nest if you move it."

Releasing her grip on the grapevine decoration, she also let go a breath of frustration. "Then what am I supposed to do? I have a date tomorrow night, and I want to make a good impression."

"You will." Wade stepped uncomfortably close. "How could he *not* be impressed?"

"You know what I mean. Imagine how odd it looks for me to be coming and going at all hours through your house."

"What's the matter?" he whispered. "Are you afraid the good people of Kinnon Falls will think we're together?"

Of course she was! But, to spare his feelings, she shook her head. "It might make Ellis feel weird."

"Here, take my key." This time he pressed the metal into the palm of her hand. His gesture clearly said he would brook no further argument on the subject. "I'll stay out of the way while you two get to know each other."

It felt so personal, so intimate, to be holding the key to his house. She'd been putting off accepting it, hoping to come up with a more acceptable solution to her bird-imposed dilemma. But that had only put them in more frequent contact as he let her and Jacob in and out of his house. Closing her fingers around the key, Geneva couldn't bring herself to meet his eyes, so she used the excuse of glancing toward the yard where Jacob played in a new sandbox Wade had built just for him.

"Your generosity in letting us cut through your home is very much appreciated." Unfortunately the birds gave her no other choice. She paused, uncertain about the propriety of putting conditions on a favor. But it was either that or be confronted with improprieties herself. When he offered to stay out of the way tomorrow night, her imagination supplied the most likely scenario—that he'd be having company of his own. "However, considering your, uh, bachelor situation, perhaps we could devise a code for when you're..." Geneva felt her cheeks flush with heat "...indisposed. Perhaps a candle in the window or a string tied around the doorknob?"

Wade ran a thumb over the shallow divot in his cheek. "Or we could wire the porch lamp to my bedsprings, and when the light flashes on and off, you'll know—"

"I should have known you'd make fun of my concern. This may not be a big deal to you, but it is a big deal where my son is concerned." Moving away from the nest and out of earshot of Jacob, she added, "The reason I moved to Kinnon Falls in the first place is because I wanted to protect him from being exposed to certain unsavory elements." The major one being the boy's father, but she wouldn't go into that now.

Wade's countenance suddenly turned serious. He leaned in as if to stress his point. Feeling dwarfed by his size, Geneva retreated a step. It didn't help much. He still took her breath away.

"It's foolish to make assumptions before you have

all the facts,'' he said. "When I want to, I can be quite...savory.''

The tone for her date with the deacon was set when Geneva failed to hear the doorbell from her apartment and Wade met Ellis at the door holding a horsewhip and wearing a devious smile. She had hoped he would be out on his own date tonight, but it looked as though he would be sticking around for the evening.

On first glance at the jeans Wade wore and the too-tight T-shirt that pulled across his chest, he looked like an eternal teenager. A well-built one. Ellis, on the other hand, was dressed for the occasion in tan slacks, a pale blue oxford shirt and a navy tie.

Jacob hid shyly behind her, pressing his face against her skirt. Except, perhaps, for the current situation with her landlord, she knew Kinnon Falls would be a wonderful place to raise her son. Discreetly studying Ellis from the den, she wondered if he might be the man with whom she would someday raise Jacob. Judging from his interaction with parishioners and the respect they held for him, he certainly appeared to be a good possibility. And if he wasn't the man for them, well, she'd keep trying until she found the right one. Never again would she marry someone who didn't fully meet her needs. And never again would she believe that she could change someone to fit her criteria of the perfect family man.

She stepped into the room, Jacob clinging like an appliqué to her leg, just as Wade was launching into his explanation about the whip.

"Our riding instructor found this in the old barn beyond the stables.'' Wade shook the coil loose and danced the worn leather across the floor. "Louis thinks it could be as much as a hundred years old."

Ellis pushed his hands into his pockets. "What are you going to do with it?"

Her nemesis flashed her a wicked smile. "At first I considered how I might use it for myself, but eventually I decided to do something a little wild and crazy."

Fearing the worst, Geneva sought to intercept the conversation and gracefully extricate Ellis to the safety and privacy of her apartment. "I don't think Wade needs to go into—"

But he was determined to finish...and most likely embarrass her.

"I was thinking I'd hang it in the Fox and Hound room at the restaurant," he said with utmost innocence. Then, raising his eyebrows at her, he rewound the whip over his hand and elbow. "What did you think I was going to do with it?"

Wade held her gaze a moment longer than necessary, breaking contact only after a flush of pink swept over her cheeks. He told himself he was only encouraging her in her wrong opinion of him because it fell in with his plan. If she thought him a wayward man, she would avoid him even if he should lose his head momentarily and attempt to flirt with her. But the real reason was that he enjoyed teasing her and watching her react with the fresh innocence of a much younger woman. He liked the way her chin dipped, revealing the embarrassment she tried not to show. He liked the way her pale brown eyes glowed with golden flecks when she confronted him about his reputation and how it might affect her child. He liked...way too much about her.

Jerking his gaze from the tight line of her soft pink lips, he addressed the man standing patiently in his living room. The deacon was a good man, and Wade was certain he'd treat Geneva right. But something deep down inside Wade nudged him, asking if that was enough. Would she be *happy* with this guy?

If this relationship went sour for her, he'd be consumed with guilt for having fixed her up with someone unsuited to her. He had to know without a doubt that they were right for each other, and to gain that certainty, he would need to know more about Deacon Tackett.

"So, what kind of car do you drive?"

Geneva sighed and narrowed her eyes at Wade to signal that she was ready to take over from here. All the while, Tackett enthusiastically filled him in about the collector-model Mustang he was restoring. Although the man's boss cam fascinated him greatly, he reluctantly acknowledged that bit of information would be of no help to Geneva. He decided a more personal question would give him a better idea of their compatibility.

Geneva turned and lifted a hand toward the den, but before she could lead her date away, Wade intercepted them. "You seem to be a man of high standards, Deacon. Tell me, what do you think is the most important attribute in a woman?"

There. That should tell him volumes about whether he was truly the right one for Geneva.

"Wade?"

The deacon touched a hand to her wrist. "That's okay, Geneva. It's a fair question." He addressed Wade much as a student answers a teacher when called on in a spelling bee. He squared his shoulders and looked him directly in the eye, fully confident in his answer. "It is written that charm is deceptive and beauty fades, but a woman who loves the Lord will be greatly praised."

"No fair," Wade said with a grin. "You took the easy way out by quoting Proverbs." It would take some thought, but Wade knew he'd have to come up with a better test.

Geneva bestowed a blistering frown on him that could have made a small child cry. "Here's another proverb for you. 'He who guards his lips guards his life.'"

This time, she hooked Tackett's elbow and practically dragged him from the room, no easy task considering that Jacob had mooched a ride on her foot. So far Wade had scored a double bogey with his line of questioning, and Geneva was calling it a game before they'd reached the eighteenth hole.

But he refused to let her off that easily. He'd impulsively hooked her up with this man, taking his reputation at face value and failing to check him out thoroughly beforehand. Wade's conscience would not allow him to stand by idly while innocent, trusting Geneva turned her heart over to someone who might not be worthy of love.

Honesty compelled him to consider that his concern about this pairing was not totally altruistic. There was something about Geneva's sweet innocence that made him want not only to protect her, but to keep her for himself. He supposed that, in an ideal world, he might have considered her his perfect match.

But this wasn't an ideal world. And he had no guarantee that Ellis was the ideal mate for Geneva.

Deacon or not, Ellis was subject to flaws just like any other man. Wade would have to find out more about this guy before the evening was out.

Chapter Three

After she'd discouraged Wade from following them into her apartment, she invited Ellis into the kitchen to keep her company while she finished preparing their dinner. She didn't know what had gotten into her landlord, but she hoped he got over it soon.

"Smells great," Ellis said as he settled into a chair at the table. "What is it?"

"Roma chicken with rice." She added the chicken and tomatoes to the sautéed onions and garlic, then covered the skillet. "This needs to simmer a little while. In the meantime, I'd love to hear about your Sunday-school class."

Just as she'd hoped, the subject was one her date enjoyed talking about, and it made a small headway toward breaking the ice between them. Even so, they were still at that awkwardly polite stage. Perhaps, by evening's end, once the effects of Wade's interrogation wore off they'd be more relaxed and better able to enjoy each other's company.

To her dismay, Wade ambled into the kitchen wearing a large grin and carrying a bottle of wine in the crook of his arm. "I noticed you were completely out of wine, so I brought you some to restock."

Flabbergasted, Geneva could only stammer, "But I don't...we're not..."

She didn't know anything about Ellis's attitude toward alcohol, but since the communion "wine" at church had actually been grape juice, she thought it safe to assume he didn't imbibe.

Wade pulled a couple of goblets from her cabinet, filled one, and handed it to Geneva. Then he poured another. "How about you, Elvis? Care for a little conversation lubrication?"

Ellis held his hand palm-out at the proffered glass. "No thanks. I don't drink."

Just as she'd thought. She had to get Wade out of here before he managed to offend Ellis further and wind up ruining her chances with this man who seemed to have so much going for him.

"No?" he persisted. Wade reached into his pocket and sidestepped her with a smile full of devious innocence. "Then how about a breath mint?"

Ellis accepted one, and Jacob took three. Great, now he was ruining her son's appetite, too.

"You have a beautiful home." Her date was obviously trying to make polite conversation.

"Thank you, Elvis. It's been in my family for generations." Geneva could have sworn he stuck out his chest as he launched into a discussion of his family's farming history. "My father was the first to give up farming for a salaried job."

She couldn't be sure, but it seemed as though a

cloud passed over his features, darkening his green eyes until they smoldered like a pine forest.

"And when the land got passed to me," he continued, "I decided a country club would be a great social center for the community and satisfy my own interests as well."

His own interests? Such as bringing the area's most elite women straight to his doorstep? Before he could get too detailed with his description of the transformation, she laid a hand on his arm and drew him into the hall.

"What are you trying to do?" she asked.

"Nothing. I'm just making conversation. Ol' Elvis was so stiff, I had to do something to loosen him up."

"His name," she said through clenched teeth, "is Ellis. Two l's, no v."

"Really? Then I won't need to ask him whether he has a white cape and a rhinestone jacket."

It was clear with that last statement that he was trying to push her hot buttons. Geneva slowly counted to three. Next time she had a date—if there was a next time—she'd make sure to meet him elsewhere. Jacob's chatter drifted to her through the closed kitchen door, and she wondered what further damage he was wreaking on her hapless guest.

"And furthermore," she continued, "it's not your job to 'loosen him up.' That's just a routine part of the dating process that we have to get through on our own."

He hooked a thumb over his belt. "I hate to tell you this, but you weren't doing a very good job of getting through it. I was beginning to feel sorry for him. The poor guy looked like he was sitting on a tack."

"Well, if you'd given me a chance—"

Wade held up his hand and lifted his chin as he sniffed the air. "Do you smell something burning?"

"My Roma chicken!"

Geneva rushed past him into the kitchen, snatched the skillet off the flame and removed the lid to inspect the damage. Pushing the spoon down into the bubbly stuff, she could tell the bottom was scorched.

"Don't stir it," Wade said over her shoulder. Leaving her for a second, he took a ceramic dish from the cabinet, just as casually as if he lived here, and brought it to her. "Pour everything in here. The scorched part will stay behind, and no one will be the wiser." To Ellis, he added, "Pretend you didn't hear me say that."

Their dinner looked okay, but the smell of scorched tomatoes lingered in the air. Geneva's shoulders drooped. "It's ruined. Maybe I should call for a pizza."

"Yeah!" Jacob enthusiastically piped in.

"They don't deliver this far out in the boonies." Wade picked up a spoon and dipped it into the sauce. "Give it a try...you'll be surprised. I do this kind of thing all the time, and it's never as bad as it smells."

"You're just saying that," she said, refusing the spoon he held to her mouth, "because you're the reason I forgot to check it."

Wade shrugged off her accusation and tasted the stuff. "See? It's not bad." He ran the tip of his tongue over his lips. "In fact, it's pretty good."

Of course Wade would insist it tasted fine. He was the culprit who'd distracted her from her cooking. By minimizing the extent of the damage, he was also minimizing his role in creating the problem.

"Fine, *you* eat it." She'd recently been paid for the prom dress she'd made for a high-school senior. Maybe she should just take Ellis to a restaurant for dinner.

"Okay, if you insist."

To her surprise, Wade added a fourth place setting to the table and started heaping the chicken and sauce over the mounds of rice on the plates. Ellis opened a napkin and spread it over his lap, and Jacob mimicked his motions.

When Wade was done serving, he pulled out the chair beside Ellis and waited for Geneva to be seated. Obviously put on the spot regarding his manners, Ellis scooted his chair back and stood politely. Still copying the older man, Jacob stood, too.

With a twist of her mouth and a warning frown at Wade, she took the seat. When he sat across from her, she knew this would not be the quiet, getting-to-know-you dinner she'd anticipated.

Ellis and Jacob returned to their chairs. When Jacob grabbed his fork and prepared to dig in, Wade reached over and took it from him. "Perhaps Mr. Tackett would like to do us the honor of saying grace."

One point for Wade. Amid the confusion of neglecting and then salvaging their dinner, she'd almost forgotten to give thanks for the food, scorched or not. But he'd saved her from embarrassing herself further in front of the deacon.

She bowed her head, and it seemed as though an eternity passed before Ellis finally said, "Amen."

Always free with his opinions, Jacob made sure to comment on the length of the prayer. "That's loooong!"

Next time, Geneva would not only meet her date elsewhere, she'd find a baby-sitter for Jacob, too.

To her relief, the meal didn't taste scorched at all. As if reading her mind, Wade gave her a smug smile. And before she could think of a suitable conversation starter, he'd launched into a three-way, male-dominated discussion about restoring classic cars.

The evening was going nothing at all the way she'd planned, thanks mostly to Wade. It was much more lively than she'd anticipated, but that was not necessarily a plus.

By the time they'd finished eating and the dishes were washed and put away, she'd learned more than she ever wanted to know about the inner workings of Ellis's 1965 vintage Mustang.

Her date was a charming man. Polite and good-looking. Intelligent and decent. She'd love to spend some quality one-on-one time with him—something that wouldn't happen on the second half of their date if it continued like the first part. And the way she figured it, Wade owed her, big time. One, for the dinner he'd mooched and, two, for being such a distraction.

She was folding the dish towel to hang it up, when Wade murmured quietly to her, "Seems to be going pretty well, don't you think?"

Her jaw went slack. He thought this was going well? Recovering her composure, she glanced over her shoulder at Ellis, who was putting away the salad dressing and directing Jacob on the best way to wipe the table. Keeping her voice low so he wouldn't overhear, she said to Wade, "I'd like to give this relationship an opportunity to grow, but that's impossible to do as a foursome.'' She paused, giving him a moment to let it sink in.

"Perhaps I could help you out," he offered. "Maybe entertain Jacob with my pinball machine for a little while so Ellis and you can, uh, *talk* without interruption. You want to put a candle in your window or tie a string around your doorknob?"

She narrowed her eyes at him. "You said *talk*. There'll be no need for a candle or a string tonight."

"Good move," he said with a wink. "Make him wait."

Geneva took a deep breath and let it out slowly. She supposed she could explain that this particular choice wasn't a dating strategy...it was who she was. But even if she did carry the discussion further with Wade, she doubted he'd understand. They lived such completely different lifestyles, and she doubted they'd ever see eye to eye on a matter such as this.

Wade glanced over his shoulder at the two of them as he led little Jacob to his den. This would give them an opportunity to talk as one adult to another, and maybe steal a kiss or two.

That last possibility bothered him more than it should have, and he didn't know why. The deacon was a nice enough guy. But something told him Ellis was wrong for Geneva.

Not that it should matter to him. She was only his tenant, for crying out loud. So why did it bother him so much to imagine them sitting knee-to-knee on her flowered couch? And why did he feel so possessive of Geneva when she was exactly the kind of woman he'd sworn many years ago to avoid?

* * *

"You're a seamstress?" Ellis crossed the living room to the sewing machine and touched some of the fabric that spilled over onto the floor.

Geneva nodded. "I do custom work. Lately most of my orders have come from a local interior designer who likes what I do with curtains. But I need to expand my customer base so I'm not totally dependent on the work she brings me."

"That dress you're wearing looks nice. Did you make it?"

"Yes. Thank you." Geneva was proud of her skill, but she doubted sewing was high on the list of topics men wanted to talk about. So, thinking the best way to "loosen him up," as Wade had put it, was to get him talking about himself, she motioned for him to have a seat on the couch and asked him about his responsibilities as deacon of the church.

He was just getting warmed up when the living-room door swung open and in walked Jacob and Wade. The older male carried a half-eaten, syrup-laden sundae, which obviously belonged to his tiny sidekick. Both wore tool belts, and both sported matching baseball caps emblazoned with the country club's distinctive logo. The hammer and screwdriver in Jacob's too-large belt had apparently pulled it so low on his narrow hips that it was now supported by leather straps that had been tied over his shoulders.

Jacob gave a little swagger and rested his hand on the hammer holster, bringing to mind a miniature John Wayne facing down a desperado.

Wade's smile faded as he noticed her and Ellis sitting together on the sofa. He moved a coaster on the coffee table and set the sticky sundae dish down on it. "I thought you two were going to be in the kitchen. We decided Jacob would help me put up that shelf you wanted, if that's all right with you."

Geneva was skeptical. He knew she wanted some time alone with Ellis. He'd even offered to watch Jacob so she could have some privacy! But, giving him the benefit of the doubt, she supposed he may have thought he wouldn't bother them if they were in the other room. She wondered if she and Ellis would be able to salvage what was left of their date.

She gave up with an impatient sigh, and in the next few minutes all three males were hard at work on the shelf in her sewing corner...Jacob holding the jar of screws, Ellis positioning the level, and Wade operating the stud finder.

How fitting, she thought, regarding the playboy's role in putting up the shelf. She paced the room as they worked, feeling like a fifth wheel.

When they were done, Geneva reined in her impatience and made appropriate noises of appreciation. She truly was grateful for the much-needed shelf, and when Jacob proudly announced, "I was *working*," she was glad he'd been included and made to feel like a big boy. But she couldn't help wishing Wade had picked a more convenient time to do it.

Urging her guest to be seated, she rejoined him on the couch and hoped the interloper would take the hint and leave.

To her relief, the landlord made a courtly bow, the tools in his belt clanking together as he did so. "We now return you to your regularly scheduled program." Then, pointing to the half-melted ice cream, he told Jacob, "Don't forget your sundae."

Her son toddled past Ellis to the coffee table and

cavalierly lifted the dessert with one hand. The heavy glass dish tilted and, in an effort to avoid an accident, her date moved to help him. But, after the boy's head-swelling experience of helping put up the shelf, he obviously considered such assistance beneath him.

"No," Jacob insisted, and attempted to pull away. That made Ellis hold tighter to steady the dish, which, in turn, prompted Jacob to give it a jerk.

It all happened so fast that Geneva never actually saw the seven flavors of ice cream and three types of syrup slosh out of the upended container...straight into Ellis's lap. And all over his tie and shirt.

"Oh, Ellis, I'm so sorry!"

Geneva set about to help clean him up, but Wade beat her to it. Removing a putty knife from his tool belt, he scraped some of the larger lumps of ice cream off the stunned man's shirt and back into the dish. As if in shock, Ellis merely sat there holding his sodden shirt away from his stomach.

And if that wasn't bad enough, Jacob's lower lip pushed out and he burst into tears. Geneva didn't know whether to comfort her son, help clean up her guest or chew out Wade for having inadvertently set up the disaster.

As for his efforts with the putty knife, Wade seemed to be making matters worse as he smeared the multicolored mixture into the light fabric. Another clump of semi-liquefied ice cream clung just below her date's belt.

Wade handed him the flat blade and stepped back. "You're on your own there, pal."

A few minutes later, after sending Jacob to his room to change into his pajamas, Geneva watched dumbfounded as the man who was no longer her possible future husband fled from the house, spinning his tires in the gravel driveway. There was no question in her mind that he wouldn't be calling her again.

Wade closed the distance between them, laying a hand on her shoulder. "I'm sorry it didn't work out the way you'd hoped."

She made no move to step away from his touch. "The man who just walked out that door could have been Jacob's stepfather someday."

Increasing the pressure on her arm, he turned her to face him. "Are you looking for a father for Jacob or a husband for you?" He tried to take her hand in his, but Geneva held tighter to the roll of paper towels she'd been carrying. Undeterred, he covered her fingers with his own. "Your son's going to grow up someday. Don't you want the man you marry to be a good match for *you?*"

"That's secondary."

If she'd focused more on pairing up with a good *father* before accepting Les's marriage proposal, perhaps she could have foreseen that he'd use an addition to their family as a flimsy excuse to turn into an unfaithful husband. With a sad shake of her head, she acknowledged in her heart she'd known even then that Les was lackluster about her desire for a large family. Foolishly, she had hoped he'd become more enthusiastic after seeing what a terrific little boy they'd brought into the world. It had been a hard lesson to learn, but Geneva knew now that it's impossible to change another person.

Removing her hand from Wade's, she fixed her gaze on the empty road, knowing she might never again find a man who possessed so many good qualities as the deacon. "Besides, I think Ellis would have been a perfect family man."

When Wade spoke, his voice was soft but firm, the very depth and warmth of it seducing her to pay attention. "Ellis is a fine person," he concurred, "but I think you can do better."

"You do? And where, pray tell, might I find this wonderful man who's supposedly sitting around waiting for me to show up in his life?"

She hated being sarcastic to anyone, even Wade, but over the course of the evening he'd managed to find her very last nerve and pluck it raw.

He opened his mouth as if starting to say something. Then, apparently thinking better of it, he merely closed the front door, blocking her view of the dust still swirling above the driveway.

Geneva moved away from him, intent on retreating to the safety of her own apartment. She stopped in the doorway separating their homes, then paced the floor in agitation.

He watched, admiring the smooth grace that was evident even in her nervous strides. He supposed he ought to apologize for his role in chasing off her suitor. An involuntary smile forced his lips upward as he took selfish satisfaction in knowing she was still unclaimed. It made no sense reacting this way when the last thing he wanted was to get involved with her.

She stopped short in her tracks. "You think this is funny, don't you?"

"No, I—"

Her eyes widened, and she stood stock-still. "You did it on purpose." She pointed the roll of paper towels at him as if it were a gun. "You broke us up! Why? Was it some kind of game? Do you give yourself points for every person whose social life you manage to demolish?''

''Of course not. I—''

''Never mind. You can save your excuse.'' She waved her arms as if to brush away what he'd been about to say. ''I can see things aren't working out here the way I'd hoped. Perhaps it would be better if I lived elsewhere.''

It was pointless to remind her this was the best place to raise her kid, and the least expensive she'd find anywhere. He could see she was doing mental calculations.

Apparently conceding defeat, she said, ''We could move in with my mother until I can afford to buy a house of my own.''

Wade crossed his arms over his chest and was inordinately pleased to see that her brown eyes darkened to near-black as her gaze followed his gesture and settled on his pecs. ''Need I remind you of your lease…and the clause wherein you agreed to be on call for Sean while I'm at work?''

She lifted her eyes to his. They brimmed with frustration. ''I'm sure you can find someone else who would agree to the same terms.''

''I don't want anyone else.''

And the truth of that bothered him. He didn't want anyone else watching out for his brother. Her mothering qualities were so strong Wade was convinced she'd care for Sean as if he were her own flesh and blood. Heck, she'd already started getting after him for eating too much convenience food and was giving him cooking lessons to ensure a healthier diet. But what got under Wade's skin was the knowledge that he also wanted her here for reasons that had nothing to do with Sean.

"You signed a one-year lease, and I expect you to fulfill your obligations." There was no doubt in his mind that she'd live up to her promise. That was why she was here. She'd told her kid she would buy them a house so he'd never have to move again, and she would do it no matter what the obstacles. "Look, the birds will be gone in a few weeks," he reminded her. "We'll both have more privacy then."

Jacob toddled up to her, ran a toy car over her knee and made a motor noise with his lips. His pajama shirt was inside out and backward. Geneva picked him up and went back to pacing. "Right. Until the next time you decide to interfere in my social life."

Wade didn't blame her for being angry with him. He hadn't intentionally set out to wreck her date, but he doubted she'd believe that now.

"Let me make it up to you."

He had no idea how he'd do that, but if he thought fast, he was sure he could come up with something, even if it was only to knock a portion off her next month's rent. Unfortunately, that felt too much like an attempt to buy her off.

If there'd been a lightbulb over her head, it would have lit up. "I know exactly how you can make restitution."

Uh-oh. She was using big words, so she must have a big payback in mind.

Geneva waited while he considered her words. What she was about to ask would help her tremendously...she only hoped he didn't think it too presumptuous. Hoping to take advantage of his guilt over ruining her evening, she widened her eyes slightly and peered up at him through her lashes.

It worked.

His expression was hooded and dark as his gaze swept over her.

He stepped closer until her eyes were level with his chin. She started to take a step backward but, remembering that her son was playing at her feet, she held her ground. Geneva tipped her head to look into the eerie green eyes that stared down at her.

"Fine," he said, his voice full of promise and danger, "However, I expect something from you in return."

"Come here, and I'll show you what I want."

Wade led Geneva into the pro shop and picked up a book that was for sale. *Golf, Then and Now.* "This one might have some pictures of what I had in mind."

He flipped through the pages, and a customer brushed past, almost knocking the book from his hands. He looked up at Geneva, and once again her pale-oak eyes nearly sent him reeling. He was powerless to their magic, which was why he had wasted no time fulfilling the promise he'd made yesterday.

"Let's go sit outside where there's more room," he suggested. More room to put a safe buffer zone between them. And perhaps once outside, the lilac blossoms would distract him from the delicious scent that beckoned him to Geneva.

With a hand to her elbow, he started to lead her to the terrace where they could drink coffee while they talked business, preferably with a table between them. But before they reached the outdoor café, he noticed Cherise having her first highball of the day.

"On second thought, that bench over on the porch would be better. We can see the nest in the eaves from there...the one that my golf pro said belongs to a pair of tufted titmice."

Once seated, she distracted him from their nearness by leaning forward to watch as the mother bird returned with a moth and fed it to her clamoring chicks. After a moment, she gave a sigh and relaxed back.

"Spring is my favorite time of year," she said, almost as if to herself. Then, noticing him watching her, she shrugged. "I'm a sucker for babies, even the ones with feathers or fur."

Wade swallowed. This was a subject he wanted to avoid at all costs. Now would be a good time for an abrupt shift in their conversation. "About those uniform designs..."

Fortunately, she was easily diverted to talking about her second-favorite subject—sewing. "The solid shirt and dark slacks your employees are currently wearing don't differentiate them from the patrons. But if you go with a common color theme—like burgundy and hunter green—and a crest on the shirt, that'll set them apart while still allowing for some kind of individuality with plaids and the cut of the clothing."

She took a deep breath before continuing, and Wade could tell she was in her element. The staff had never cared much for the color or quality of uniforms they'd been provided, so when Geneva had asked him to recommend her services to the people who booked the pavilion or clubhouse for parties and weddings, this had seemed like the perfect solution to her demand for "restitution." He scratched her back and she scratched—

Wade shook the image from his head. No sense tantalizing himself for something that never would be. Never *could* be.

So why had he demanded a favor of her in return? He hadn't specified what it would be because he himself hadn't figured that out. Maybe he'd ask her to do a little something extra for Sean…anything as long as he didn't redeem the favor for himself.

"Then top off the ensemble with a beret," she continued, "and you're all set."

A golf cart putted past in the distance, and the driver lifted a hand in greeting. She returned Sean's friendly salute, then turned back to Wade and gave him a smile that made him want to reach for her. Made him want to push back her wild curls and nuzzle the pulse spot on her neck, all the while inhaling the beguiling scent that reminded him of fresh-baked cookies.

Only half listening to what she'd said, Wade rose from the bench and paced the porch planks. "Isn't it almost time for you to pick up Jacob from his play date at church?"

"Not yet," she said, apparently unaware that he was trying to get rid of her. "He's scheduled to stay until noon."

A movement under one of the table umbrellas caught his attention. To his dismay, Cherise rose from her chair and turned in his direction, her large-brimmed hat threatening to sail off on the breeze that teased them with hints of an impending afternoon shower.

"Wade Matteo, I've been expecting you to call," the woman said as she stepped off the brick terrace. Apparently surprised to see Geneva, Cherise gave her a quick once-over, then dismissed her with a toss of her bottle-blond head. "Have you been avoiding me, you naughty man?"

Geneva rose to her feet, the only clue that she felt Cherise's cut being the white-knuckle grip with which she held the book they'd been perusing earlier. "I think we've just about finished our *meeting*." Darting a glance in Cherise's direction, she added, "I'll draw up some sketches and meet with you again in a few days."

Wade grinned as he took in her erect posture and the brisk clip of her words. There was no mistaking her intent. She sought to make it clear that their relationship was merely business.

Her chin tilted higher than usual, the gesture even more telling than the hurt in her eyes that she'd felt the sting of Cherise's snub. He couldn't let her leave like this. Crooking a hand through her arm, he prevented her escape.

"Cherise, let me introduce you to my neighbor, Geneva Jensen."

The older woman sniffed and repositioned the purse strap on her shoulder. "Charmed to meet you." She folded her arms at her waist, the action and coolness of her tone belying her words. Then, moving to Wade's side, she laid a hand on his arm and spoke in a hush. "I've put off responding to two invitations to the charity ball in hopes that you would ask me."

She flashed him a brilliant, red-lipped smile, and Wade cringed as she laid her other hand intimately on his side. He had planned to ask her, and it certainly would be the smart thing to do. She was already primed for him to tap what she had to offer. But the thought of spending an entire evening in her company filled him with dread.

Reminding himself that this was about more than his own desires, he steeled himself to be gracious.

"That's a most tempting suggestion—"

Geneva cleared her throat. "It was nice meeting you." She pulled away from Wade to make her exit, but he impulsively stopped her with a hand to her waist.

"—however, Ms. Jensen has already asked me to accompany her."

Geneva took a quick breath in what sounded suspiciously like a gasp. "I'm not going to—"

"Take no for an answer?" He gave her a warning smile and pressed her tightly against him. Then, to Cherise who had stepped away in an obvious miff, he added conspiratorially, "As you can see, she's quite persistent."

Geneva squirmed within his unexpected embrace. She should have known that her requested favor would backfire, especially when Wade became involved in it.

She needed to straighten this out right away, before rumors started flying. Geneva opened her mouth to speak, but Cherise had the first say.

After another, this time disdainful, assessment, the other woman said to Wade, "She doesn't look like your usual type."

Geneva thought she detected a hint of amusement pulling at one corner of Wade's mouth. "She's anything but usual," he declared.

With an imperious flout, the other woman

swooshed past them, pausing only long enough to toss a word of caution to Geneva. "I'd better warn you, honey, he's only after one thing. And, truthfully, you don't look like you have enough to satisfy him."

Chapter Four

"**W**ell, thank you very much," Geneva said after
Cherise was gone. She made no effort to hide the
sarcasm that practically dripped from her voice.
"Once word gets out that I'm going to this charity
ball with you—which I'm *not,* by the way—I'll never
be able to meet a nice guy."

He politely ignored her unintended insult. Following his lead, she decided it was probably best at this
point to ignore Cherise's comment that she didn't
have enough to satisfy a man like Wade. She hadn't
been able to satisfy Les either, which was his excuse
for splurging their house savings on trips and gifts for
his mistress. Geneva felt her lip quiver, and she
fought the wave of anger and self-blame that threatened to erode her remaining shred of self-confidence.

"Aw, come on, it's not that bad." Wade slung an
arm over her shoulder in a gesture that was meant to
comfort but that only served to make her more aware
of the heat of his body and the hard-ridged planes of

his torso. "Be seen with me at the charity ball, maybe even get your picture on the society page, and the next thing you know, all kinds of men will be asking you out."

"That's the problem." She tried to pull away from him lest anyone find them in this compromising position, but his fingers squeezed the upper part of her arm, the action bringing her so close she could feel his breath against her hair. "The men who would ask me out because I dated you are exactly the type I want to avoid." She paused, belatedly realizing how that must have sounded. "No offense intended."

"None taken." He said it so quickly that she wondered if he had indeed taken umbrage at her comment. "Tell you what. You accompany me to the charity ball, and I'll make up for ruining your date with Ellis."

She held up a hand. "Never mind. I'll find a way to meet men on my own."

But he wouldn't hear of it.

"You promised me a favor."

"That's ridiculous! I don't owe you a thing. Or have you already forgotten about the ice-cream sundae you gave my son to pour all over poor Elvis? I mean Ellis."

Good grief, now he even had her calling the fellow by the wrong name. She was becoming rattled...a condition that often happened whenever she was near her landlord.

"I didn't tell him to dump it in the deacon's lap. That was his own idea." The smile that peeked through his expression of supposed sincerity let her know that he wasn't altogether remorseful about what had happened the other night. "You asked for a favor, as payback for the, um, mishap. That has been accomplished by my hiring you to create new uniforms for my staff.''

"Then let's just cancel the whole deal, and we'll both be off the hook."

But it didn't do any good to try to reason with him. He released her, not from their bargain, but from the overly familiar grip he had on her shoulders. To her annoyance, the distance between them now seemed like an aching chasm that left her feeling even more alone than when Les had taken off with her hopes, dreams and money.

"No way. We made a deal, and we're going to stick to it. When I make a promise, it's forever." His whole demeanor was that of an autocrat who had declared the subject closed. "You'll be going with me to the charity ball. And to show you my gratitude, I'll introduce you to an eligible doctor. Very highly respected. Everyone likes him."

"A doctor?" The previous hookup he'd arranged had been a disaster because she'd made the mistake of holding the date on Wade's turf. Maybe it wouldn't have been so bad if she and Ellis had gone someplace neutral. Considering the high caliber of this new prospect, Geneva decided it would be hasty to reject Wade's suggestion out of hand.

"A pediatrician." Her enthusiasm must have shown, judging by his grin of acknowledgment. "Meet me here at noon Saturday. He has a standing reservation for lunch on the terrace after his eighteen holes."

The carrot was so enticing Geneva couldn't refuse it. A man of high esteem in the community, successful in his business as proven by his gold-star membership in the country club, and a pediatrician, to boot. What more could she ask for?

Okay, so maybe she was a twinge shallow. "Is he good-looking?"

"A modern-day Cary Grant."

With a prospect that good, she'd date the devil himself...which, come to think of it, were the terms of this deal.

Wade winked and held out his hand to bind their arrangement with a shake.

Gee, and she'd never realized the devil had such glittering green eyes.

Geneva finished vacuuming the last of the spiderweb from Jacob's bedroom window and returned the appliance to the hall storage closet.

When she came back to the room decorated with *Cat in the Hat* characters, she sighed with satisfaction at the cheerful environment her son would wake up in for the next few years. She'd had such fun sewing the quilted cover on his bed and making the coordinating lampshade cover. Perhaps by the time he was ready to start kindergarten, she'd have saved enough for a down payment on a house of their own. By then he'd probably be ready to give up the Dr. Seuss characters that adorned his room and switch to a race-car theme, or perhaps cowboys or soccer.

She crossed over the rug she'd braided while she'd been pregnant with her son and remembered it as one of the happiest times of her life. With any luck, she'd get pregnant again—married first, of course—and fill their home with brothers and sisters for Jacob. A smile captured her lips as she returned the screen to the window and latched it shut. What she wouldn't give to braid rugs for a half-dozen babies and sew rag dolls and baby gowns for each child. Perhaps they'd have brown eyes like hers and Jacob's. Or maybe blue or gray, depending on what their father looked like.

Unbidden, an image of forest-green eyes framed by thick black lashes popped into her mind. She immediately tried to sweep it away, just as she had eradicated the spiderweb from the window to ease her son's fears. The problem was this particular image kept coming back, and she found it much more terrifying than any spider could ever be.

The screen safely secured, she turned and noticed the plastic dump truck Jacob had been playing with earlier. He'd said something about watching cartoons, but he was probably ready for his morning snack by now.

She stepped into the living room, but the television was off. Maybe he had toddled into the kitchen to help himself to a banana. She checked her watch. That was odd. He would never miss Bugs Bunny, not even for a snack.

A check of the kitchen revealed he wasn't there. No sign of him in her room or the bathroom either. A panicky knot clutched at Geneva's throat.

"He must be hiding." She said the words aloud as if to convince herself of their truth. The last place she'd seen him was in his bedroom, so she started her search there. "Jacob? Come out, sweetie, so Mommy can see you."

By the time she'd checked the rest of the rooms— under furniture, in closets, and even in the laundry hamper—her voice was tinged with fear. Where could he be? It wasn't like him to willfully disobey her when she called.

She recounted this morning's events, trying to re-call everything that had happened in the last ten minutes. Spiderweb, cartoons...*Sean!* Their neighbor had been outside on the riding lawn mower and had called to them as he passed by the open window.

Oh, no. Could Jacob have scuttled out the window while she was putting the vacuum away? It was a long drop to the ground below, but if he landed just right, he could have avoided injury. Unlatching the screen again, she poked her head out the window and saw her young neighbor maneuvering among a stand of maple trees. Straight ahead was the golfer's water hazard that separated Wade's private domain from the country-club grounds. To her left, the footbridge that connected the two loomed like a child magnet. Could he have...?

Her head throbbed, and a wave of dizziness swept over her before she realized she'd stopped breathing. A deep gulp of air restored her, but her heart hammered against her ribs and her tongue stuck like sand to the roof of her mouth.

"Jacob?" Her voice cracked, and she cleared her throat before trying again. *"Jacob!"* Unfortunately, her trembling scream was drowned out by the lawn mower's roar as Sean made another line past the house.

Dropping the screen, Geneva ran through the apart-ment. Without even pausing for her customary warn-ing knock on the door that led to Wade's den, she whirled into his house and ran for the front door. Au-tomatically, she called out her landlord's name. Maybe he'd help her with the search.

"Yeah," he called from one of the back rooms.

In a split-second decision, she changed directions

to head down the hall. Unfortunately, the message didn't reach her body until the whole force of her weight fell on her right knee, wrenching it as she veered left. "Wade!"

"I'm in here."

She stumbled toward his voice, ignoring the pain that seized her knee. The words came tumbling out even before she'd reached his room. "It's all my fault. I left the screen out, and now Jacob's…" Following the noise of the television, she lurched into his room and stopped cold at what she saw. "…gone."

Relief surged through her every fiber as the image before her registered in her brain. There on the king-size bed the two males lounged like lions after a feast. Each relaxed against several plush pillows, the remote control and an empty box of sweetened cereal on the bed between them. Like Wade, her son sprawled with hands behind his head, evidence of his snack clinging to his shirt as Bugs Bunny blared at them from the television set across the room. Jacob's bare legs were crossed, right ankle over left, just like Wade's.

Her landlord held up a hand, his attention fixed straight ahead. "Just a moment. This is the best part."

A couple of seconds of comical music followed as Geneva stared in stunned disbelief at the two of them.

They burst into laughter at the same time, and the program cut to a commercial. "Can you believe that ricochet shot?" Wade asked, leaning toward his new-found TV buddy. *"Pyongg!"* he said, slicing his hand through the air. "Just like that!"

Jacob grinned and mimicked his motion. *"Pyongg!"* Then, discovering an errant cereal square on his chest, he picked it off and popped it into his mouth.

"I've been looking all over for you!" Geneva rushed to the bed and wrapped her arms around her son, wishing she could always keep him within her protective embrace. "Please don't ever go off without asking me first. You could have gotten hurt, and I wouldn't have known where to find you."

He squirmed, but she didn't loosen her hold. The adrenaline that had surged through her earlier now sought release. When Jacob squeaked under the pressure, she released him and focused her energy on his mentor, who was pushing buttons on the remote to lower the volume.

"I've been looking all over for him." Despite her best efforts to control her emotions, tears pooled in her eyes. She wiped them away with the back of her hand. "I thought he might have gone outside and fallen in the…" She swung her arm toward the back of the house, and a sob broke as she voiced the terror that had filled her just moments before. "…lake!"

"Shh!" Jacob put a finger to his lips, then clambered off the bed to sit on the floor, closer to the source of his entertainment.

"Oh, Gen, I'm so sorry." Wade wasted no time coming to her. He knelt on the mattress before her, capturing her hands in his. "Jacob told me you were working. I thought you'd sent him over here to get him out of your hair for a while."

She shook her head. "I would *never* do that!"

His grip tightened on her fingers. "Never try to get him out of your hair?" He paused, and when he spoke again his voice was low and tight. "Or never send him to *me?*"

Geneva sniffed. Both, actually, but now that she knew her son was safe, she could see there'd been no real harm done. Unless, of course, she counted the sweetened cereal.

"Look!" Jacob pointed at the television screen. *"Pyongg!"*

It was clear Jacob liked Wade. Her son had no idea that their landlord's social life was so different from their own. All he knew was that Wade doled out generous portions of attention, not to mention edible treats, on him, which was something his own father had never done. She couldn't blame him for liking the man. What kid wouldn't, given those conditions?

And now she had gone and insulted Wade…again. He'd only been trying to lend her a helping hand, and look how she'd repaid him. The typically charming glint in his green gaze was gone, and in its place she saw… She wasn't sure what she saw in the multihued flecks. Disappointment maybe? Regret? Possibly even a little fear?

"I meant I would never dump my child on anyone, especially not without asking first."

His murky sea-colored eyes lightened until they reminded her of the soft fabric she had chosen for the new quilt she'd just started.

Wade moved over to the spot Jacob had vacated, allowing one leg to dangle beside the bed and folding the other so that Geneva sat in the triangle between them.

"Jake's always welcome to watch Saturday-morning cartoons with me." He pushed a dark curl behind her shoulder and allowed his finger to trace her collarbone, then upward along her pulse until his big callused hand cupped the curve of her jaw. "You, too."

His voice rasped, husky and inviting. Against her will, she imagined the three of them propped against those comfortable pillows, sharing Choco-Bites and laughter. Just like a family. Just like the family she had imagined having with Les. But that wasn't possible. Not with her ex-husband. And certainly not with Wade.

Reining in her miscreant thoughts, she focused instead on the matter that had brought her here in the first place. Her heart had only now slowed to whipstitch speed.

"Next time he watches cartoons with you," she said, conveniently leaving herself out of the possible scenario, "let's check with each other directly. I can't bear to think of what might have—"

She broke off, unable to finish the thought. Jacob meant everything to her, and no matter how many brothers and sisters he eventually ended up with someday, that love would never diminish. Her eyes burned, and the space above her nose felt tight. To her embarrassment, she could tell an ugly cry was coming on. One of those red-nosed, bleary-eyed, chest-deep-moaning kind of cries. The kind that squeezes off your throat and burns a hole in your soul.

Geneva tried to breathe, tried to suppress the emotion that swept over her, but the stress of the last couple of months—the arrival of the long-delayed divorce papers, uprooting Jacob only to start all over from scratch, compromising her privacy because of a couple of nesting birds, renting from a man of questionable personal repute, almost losing Jacob to God knows what kind of dangers that lurked outside, and now a throbbing knee—crippled the very control she tried to summon.

"Hey, it's okay now." Wade reached for her, pulling her into his arms until her head rested against his chest.

Ensconced within the shelter of his strong arms, with his knee braced comfortingly against her back, Geneva's determination buckled, giving way to deep sobs that wracked her body. It seemed as though a cork had popped loose as her disappointments and fears surged forth like champagne foam.

"I'm so—" She couldn't even say the word *embarrassed,* her tears were flowing so fast and heavy.

Wade stroked her hair, letting his touch linger at her temple. She could feel the warmth from his hand as it passed over her cheek. Automatically her arms went up around his neck as she sought solace from the pain that flowed out of her.

"Let it all out," he encouraged, and the sympathy in his tone elicited another geyser of tears. All the while, he held her, patting her back and murmuring soothing sounds.

As the release started to subside, she became aware of Jacob coming up between their entwined arms. Leaning in, he peered into her face and asked in his concerned, sweet baby voice, "You okay?"

Spent from the emotional exertion, Geneva lifted her head from Wade's shirt. She tried to wipe the moisture from her eyes but only succeeded in smearing the salty trail across her cheeks. "Yes, honey. I'll be fine soon."

That said, and the latest commercial over, the boy bunny-hopped back to the foot of the bed to finish his cartoon.

Wade opened his shirt and lifted one of the front flaps. Using a corner of the beige muslin, he erased the wet streaks from her face, then passed her the dry side to dab the corners of her eyes.

Geneva leaned forward, inhaling the faint mixture of aftershave, maleness and Choco-Bites. Under the gaping placket, a light sprinkling of soft black hairs feathered across his sun-browned chest, trailing downward in a narrow path to a place she had no business thinking about.

"Thank you." She closed the folds of fabric over his bare skin, but it did little to eradicate the vision of his lean-muscled body from her mind.

"You might fool him," Wade said, his voice rumbling deep in his chest, "but I know better."

His gaze held hers, the spruce depths probing into her thoughts, unearthing them as easily as a child digs up sand crabs at the beach. As much as she'd tried to hide the truth even from herself, she wasn't okay. Not yet. She'd tried to conceal her fears and uncertainties behind a facade of competence—cooking, cleaning, sewing and being an overall ace mother—but he'd seen them. And he still looked at her with a hunger that no amount of Roma chicken or homemade pies could fill.

She lifted her chin, intent on trying to repair the crack in her mask, to cover it with smooth words meant to assure them both that she was fine. Or soon would be. That her crying spell was a temporary aberration. But he had already seen the void in her heart.

Stopping her protest with a low sound that made her think of a growling cougar, he leaned in to her. She didn't have the time or presence of mind to resist what she knew was coming, and once his lips touched hers, she couldn't bring herself to pull away.

His mouth was warm and soft, covering hers with an ease that seemed more natural than practiced. He slid his hands around her waist, and Geneva leaned into him, hooking her arms over his massive shoulders. He dragged his hands over her ribs, his thumbs lazily brushing the sides of her breasts.

Geneva gasped, the pleasure associated with the sensation catching her by surprise more than the shock at his bold familiarity.

He kissed her again, this time lingering gently, giving more than he took. It was a new experience for Geneva…to be cherished with a mere touch. And, rather than fulfill her, it set her to craving more. It awakened something that had been lying dormant inside for a long time.

The need, both physical and spiritual, that arose within her, prompting her to return his kiss with an unfamiliar ache for more, consumed her with its urgency. She longed to sink onto the thick comforter and let him trap her beneath his hard, tanned body. She wanted to remove his shirt and run her fingertips over his torso, teasing the soft tickly hairs and relishing the ripples of muscle and ribs. Her body wanted his…cried out to it to join her and fill her long-neglected need. And her heart wanted the rest of him to take her and make her his. She gazed up into the smoldering green depths of his eyes and saw a brief moment of sadness in them before his expression closed over.

As he pulled away from her and refastened his shirt, a gust of cool air burst from the air-conditioning vent, emphasizing the loss of warmth she'd had in his embrace.

"I'm sorry," he said, rising from the bed. "That won't happen again." It sounded as though he was saying it as much for his own benefit as for hers.

She smoothed her hair and glanced over at her son who hadn't moved from his spot in front of the television. She'd had no business behaving that way. Not with Wade, and certainly not on his bed. Imagine what it would do to her reputation if her son innocently commented that his mommy had been kissing Wade in bed.

Wade turned his back to her and crossed to the closet where he retrieved a pair of slacks and a fresh shirt. He didn't know what had got into him, prompting him to kiss Geneva like that. His finely honed survival skills had warned him away from her, but something stronger had urged him to quiet the panic that beat in her breast and, ultimately, to taste the rosy pink lips that had been tempting him since the first day he saw her. Unfortunately, that small sampling did nothing to quell his desire for her. Rather, it taunted him with her sweetness and the knowledge that even greater treasures lay hidden beneath the surface…if only he was willing to take them in his grasp.

But what could he give her in return? Far less than she wanted. Or deserved. It would be much kinder, to both of them, if he kept his hands, eyes and lips off her. And the best way to do that was to take her out of circulation. Place her out of his reach.

Tossing the clothes onto the bed beside her, Wade realized his actions seemed abrupt. He had no desire to hurt her, but he couldn't continue leading her on either. Not if he intended to maintain his long-held vow of bachelorhood. And not if he wanted to spare her the pain that was sure to come if she got close to him.

"If you want to meet that doctor," he said, his voice sounding unnaturally harsh, "we'd better head down to the clubhouse soon…before either of us does something we'll regret."

With any luck, maybe the doctor would be able to give her what she was looking for.

The "modern-day Cary Grant" turned out to look more like a young Henry Kissinger. He wasn't unattractive, but he didn't seem like the leading-man type she'd been led to expect.

"It's a pleasure to meet you," the bespectacled man said, rising from his chair and extending a hand in welcome. "Won't you join me?"

She accepted his invitation and took the seat next to him after helping Jacob into a chair. Wade settled himself into the remaining seat, directly across from her.

"Geneva, this is the pediatrician I was telling you about," Wade said, finishing the introduction. "Dr. Grant works in the medical building on Derwent Avenue."

Geneva's eyes flew open. "Dr. *Grant?*" Slanting a suspicious glance at Wade, she asked the doctor, "Is your first name, by any chance, Cary?"

He smiled and adjusted the heavy-rimmed glasses on his nose. "Carrington, actually, but it got shortened to Cary."

Geneva twisted her mouth to one side. Cary was a pleasant enough fellow, but she didn't like being misled by her landlord. Before she could comment, a waitress showed up at the table. Wade sent her away with an order for three Cokes.

"I seldom let Jacob have colas," she told him pointedly. This was the second time today that her son would have junk food, and the day was barely half over. "The caffeine disturbs his sleep."

Unremorseful, he gave the boy a mock punch in the shoulder. "Aw, what's it going to hurt? It'll be out of his system in a few hours."

She turned to the doctor, hoping he'd use his authority and side with her. The man shrugged apologetically. "He's right. Perhaps this once won't hurt."

Wade leaned back in his chair, the knit material stretching across his chest and a subtle smile giving evidence that he'd noticed her awareness. "Why don't you show the doctor your knee? Maybe he can suggest something that'll make it feel better."

Dr. Grant pasted on a sympathetic frown, obviously his well-practiced bedside expression. "What did you do to your knee? I noticed you were limping earlier."

Great, now he would think she was mooching for free medical advice. "Oh, it's nothing. Just twisted it a little."

Fortunately, he didn't pursue the subject further. If she wanted a chance at building a relationship with this man—or any man for that matter—she'd best get Wade out of the picture. Fast.

"Don't you have to check on the golf course or book a tennis tournament? Or something?"

He smiled knowingly but didn't move a muscle. The rat.

"No. My employees are capable of handling things without interference from me. Which is fine as far as

I'm concerned because that leaves more time for recreation.''

She didn't even want to think what kind of recreation he might be referring to.

The waitress brought their drinks, and Jacob had downed almost half of it before she moved the glass out of his reach. He screwed up his face and announced, ''My stomach hurts.''

''Then quit bouncing in your chair.''

Her son settled back and exchanged weary glances with Wade.

If she'd had any idea of impressing the doctor, that possibility was now moot. Besides, she'd tried to make a good impression on Ellis Tackett, and look where that had gotten her. Perhaps it would be better to take a different approach this time and focus on checking *him* out. As a pediatrician, odds were good that he liked children. But she'd feel better knowing that he liked *her* child in particular. Perhaps she could get the two talking and observe how well they interacted.

''Jacob, why don't you tell Dr. Grant what you made at day care yesterday?''

The boy rose on his knees so he could see above the table. When he opened his mouth to speak, a gargantuan belch poured forth that would have done any two-hundred-pound, beer-guzzling redneck proud.

''Jacob! What do you have to say for yourself?''

He placed a hand on his tummy. ''I feel better now.''

Fortunately, the doctor seemed unfazed by her son's lapse in manners. Perhaps in his occupation he'd seen and heard much worse. She hoped so.

To her annoyance, Wade did a poor job of hiding

his amusement. "I'd say that registers a six on the Richter scale."

"Are you *sure* you don't have someplace else to go?"

He grinned and spread his arms wide. "I'm as free as a bird."

And just as inconvenient. Perhaps even more so than the nesting pair that had interfered with her lifestyle for the past week.

He leaned forward and finished off the rest of his beverage. Then, setting the glass down with a decisive thump, he declared, "Look, it's impossible for you two to get to know each other better, what with all the distractions around here. What do you say I babysit Jacob sometime while you talk over a nice quiet meal?"

Geneva placed her hands in her lap, wishing she could just disappear from this embarrassing situation. He was putting the poor man on the spot, practically forcing him to ask her out. "I'd say that's very presumptuous of you," she told Wade in her chilliest tone.

"Actually," said Dr. Grant, "I've been trying to think of a way to steer the conversation in that direction."

"See?" Wade said with a triumphant smile. "Everything's working out just fine. Now all you have to do is make him some of your famous Roma chicken and—"

"I would, but my current sewing project is hogging the kitchen table." It wouldn't be that difficult or time-consuming to clear it off, but they didn't need to know that. There was no way she'd invite him over and risk a repeat of her previous dating fiasco.

"No problem," Dr. Grant told her. "If you like steak, I know of this great restaurant on the other side of town. Cassidy's even has live music."

"It sounds delightful."

Wade scowled and rubbed his jaw. "I don't think it's such a good idea. That place is—"

"Exactly where we'll go," she interrupted.

"Great." Dr. Grant handed her his card. "I'll be out of town for a medical convention next weekend, but perhaps we could get together after I return. Call me and we can set up a time."

"Perfect." She took the proffered card and tucked it into her purse.

From the look Wade shot her, she could tell his opinion was that this arrangement was anything but perfect.

Chapter Five

Dragging the deck chair closer to Jacob's bedroom window, Geneva flopped down into it and gazed up at the solitary star that gleamed faintly in the early-night sky. Jacob had been asleep for almost an hour and it was doubtful he'd wake up before morning, but she wanted to be close enough to hear him just in case.

She closed her eyes for a moment, wondering for the hundredth time if she'd ever be able to make sense of today's events. It bothered her that she'd reacted so strongly to Wade's kiss. It had started out naturally enough, with him offering a comforting arm. And in retrospect, she wasn't surprised that he'd taken it to the next level with a kiss that affected her all the way to her toes. He was a notorious playboy, after all. But she had been surprised by the brief glimmer of emotion displayed in his eyes. There was no mistaking that he'd been as deeply affected by it as she had been. But then the abruptness that followed had led her to wonder if he thought *she* had initiated the kiss…a ridiculous idea, but he'd sure acted annoyed with her afterward. And he sure seemed eager to foist her off on the doctor.

Guitar music drifted across the lake, above the calling of crickets and tree toads, and a woman's beautiful soprano voice floated like a gossamer cloud in the night air. Turning in the direction from which it came, Geneva noticed a small crowd gathered at the water's edge on the other side of the lake. Each person lifted a candle as the words of "The Wedding March" affirmed the marriage that was about to take place.

Japanese lanterns illuminated the couple, and Geneva peered through the rapidly deepening dusk at the white-gowned bride. Wistfulness enveloped her as she gazed upon the blond woman and imagined herself in the lacy confection, proclaiming her vows to the dark-haired man at her side.

Lifting her eyes heavenward in a silent prayer, she asked once again for her request to be fulfilled. Then, noticing the star was still there, she doubled her chances by wishing for just the right man to show up in her life. Could Dr. Grant be the ideal man who would someday stand at the edge of the lake with her? If not, then maybe—

"I thought I'd find you here." Wade moved a chair beside hers and lowered himself into it. "Ten to one you're sitting there dreaming of the day you'll walk down the aisle with your own Prince Charming."

Geneva gave him an unladylike snort. "Not all women are hung up on such ideas."

"Maybe not, especially not the ones I prefer but you sure fit the bill," he said smugly. "I'll bet you're even thinking you might like a nighttime wedding as well, with the moonlight bathing your skin and a veil of darkness hiding the look of terror on the poor groom's face."

She turned to face him and immediately wished she hadn't. The wedding lights that glimmered off the surface of the water illuminated his most prominent features—smooth straight nose, dark-rimmed eyebrows and high cheekbones—and shadowed his eyes and temples. In the evening haze he seemed more handsome, more enticing, and more dangerous than ever before.

"There you go generalizing about men, just because you have some irrational fear of commitment."

"There's nothing at all irrational about my choice to stay single. And, for what it's worth, commitment has nothing to do with my decision."

She narrowed her eyes at him and was about to ask what he meant by that when he cut her off by handing her a white square of paper.

"Here's a customer for you. The lady booked the reception hall for a wedding next month because her fiancé's new promotion requires that they move to Europe right afterward. None of the dress shops will work with her on such short notice, so I told her about you."

"Thanks," she said, resisting the urge to run inside and phone the woman right away. There would be enough time for that tomorrow.

"You don't have to call her now," he said as if reading her mind. "Sit out here and finish enjoying your fantasy."

For a moment she thought he might be arrogant enough to picture himself in the middle of that so-called fantasy. And then she remembered his assumption that she wanted a nighttime wedding.

"For your information," she said, choosing to respond to the latter of the two possibilities, "I want an afternoon wedding. My future husband and I will enter into marriage in the full light of day, with our eyes wide open." Unlike her first marriage, in which she'd seen her husband as she *had wanted* him to be, rather than the way he truly was.

"Interesting. It's my far-from-knowledgeable opinion that marriage is supposed to be an opportunity for discovery. A time to learn things about each other you'd never known before."

"Maybe so," she concurred, "but sometimes those discoveries can be unpleasant, and possibly even threaten the relationship. I'd rather know about them before taking the big step."

"A prenuptial agreement? Funny, but I don't picture you as the cynical type."

"I wasn't referring to a prenup. I was talking about full disclosure, being totally honest with each other so both can make an informed decision."

Wade turned away from her, but not before she saw the flash of anger cross his handsome features, and he rose from his chair to pace the planks of the deck. When at last he paused to lean his forearms on the railing, he didn't look at her but rather gazed past her toward his brother's darkened apartment. An early bird, Sean had already gone to bed and would be up before sunrise, so she wondered why Wade's attention was fixed in that direction.

"Sometimes there are things people can't disclose heading into a marriage...things they don't even know themselves until the knot is tied and children have arrived. And by then it's too late." He blew out a breath. "And people's lives are changed forever."

A long silence passed between them. There was a lot about Wade Matteo she didn't understand, the greatest of which was his opinions on fidelity and marriage. Whatever had caused him to form those beliefs was apparently rooted deep in his past, and she had no intention of prying into matters that didn't concern her. But there was a different matter, one which involved both of them, that she needed to clarify.

"About this morning," she began.

He straightened and faced her. "Look, if it's about the junk food, I've already apologized for that. I had no idea Jacob would miss his nap because he was so pumped up on sugar and caffeine."

"It's not about that." Her tone must have alerted him to the seriousness of the subject, for he straightened, his posture as erect as if he were staring down a firing squad. "It's about what happened between us. Between you and me."

He relaxed. "Oh that." He glanced left and right, a grin lifting one corner of his mouth. "Don't tell me your father is standing nearby with a shotgun."

Geneva launched herself out of the chair, ignoring the lingering throbbing in her knee. "That's exactly what I want to clear up. After you kissed me, you acted like I had...had *imposed* myself on you."

Like she'd wanted a relationship with him. The absurdity of that notion caused her to place her hands on her hips in a posture of defensiveness.

He smiled, and she caught the flash of his even white teeth. "It wasn't the first time that's happened to me."

"You arrogant, self-centered—"

"Carousing, decadent," he offered helpfully.

"—narcissistic, hedonistic—"

"Don't forget adorable and cuddly."

"—randy scoundrel. You kissed *me!*"

"If that's what you want to tell your friends, I'll go along with your story."

She'd better calm herself down. She could actually feel her nostrils flaring. Taking a deep breath, she steadied herself and shot home her final bullet. "And you *liked* it"

There, let him deny that!

He approached her, his long strides closing the distance between them. It was all Geneva could do to keep from retreating as he trespassed on her comfort zone. "As much as you may wish to think otherwise," he said, his voice low and husky, "it was just an attempt to soothe a frightened friend." He stared down at her, the green in his eyes appearing black in the dim light. "I'm sorry if that disappoints you, but that's the way it was."

Ignoring his last comment, she repeated her point, emphasizing it with an accusing finger tapping his chest. "You liked it."

Wrong move. He captured her hand and held it there to keep her from pulling away. She could feel the *thump-thump* of his heart beating against her knuckles.

"Your belief in fairy-tale marriages and such," he said, the scorn evident in his words, "is giving you foolish romantic notions. I suggest you wise up and see the situation for what it really was."

"Yes, I do believe in fairy-tale marriages," she declared, "but that has nothing to do with what passed between us this morning.'' She tried to ignore the heat that sparked as he stroked the sensitive curve between her thumb and forefinger, sending tiny tingles up her arm and straight to her heart. ''I just think it would be best to address the issue directly to prevent it from causing us further problems.''

''Things are seldom as they seem,'' he said significantly. ''You were mistaken.''

''I know what I saw.'' And she knew what she felt, but she wasn't going to admit that. Not to him. And not at this close range.

''You want proof?'' Pulling her captive hand to his side, he pressed it there while his other hand reached out to cup the back of her head. ''You want me to show you that what you think you saw was all a figment of your vivid imagination?''

Without waiting for a response, Wade tangled his fingers in her rumpled curls, exerting gentle pressure until her face was tipped upward to him, her throat arched in provocative invitation. He knew he must be crazy to venture back into such dangerous territory, but he had a point to prove…as much to himself as to her.

The instant his mouth touched hers, he knew he'd made a mistake. The soft fullness of her lips parted slightly, and he took advantage of her momentary acquiescence, easing into the forbidden chamber and tasting the honeyed sweetness. A sigh escaped her, and he caught it in his mouth and breathed it back to her as they fed and teased each other with their very essence. He was lost in her, lost in the dream he could never claim. And the knowledge of it hammered in the pit of his soul, creating a disturbance the likes of which he'd never known before.

It wasn't supposed to happen this way. It wasn't supposed to feel this good, being with the one woman in the world who could hurt him more than anyone else. Being with the woman whose fragile heart he would most definitely break with his inability to give her what she needed.

He should stop this now…stop it before either of them fell into the bleak abyss that surely awaited them if they took that one wrong step over the edge.

When he reluctantly ended the kiss, he caught the misty warmth in her eyes…the very same look she had accused him of wearing after their first kiss. Quickly, he turned away so she wouldn't see it reflected in his own gaze.

But it was too late.

"I was right," she said, her voice a mere whisper. "You *do* want to live the fairy-tale as much as I do."

Wade recoiled as if she'd physically punched him.

"No!" He turned so she wouldn't see the lie he'd been telling everyone, including himself, for years. Focusing on the newly married couple across the lake, he shook his hand in vehement denial. "If I'd wanted that, I'd be standing over there beside the bride right now."

Geneva moved next to him and rested her elbows on the deck railing. Too close. Even so, he stood his ground.

"What happened?" she asked softly.

"You're not going to let this drop, are you?"

Her silence told him he may as well give her the information she wanted. Maybe it would scare her off, shake her belief that he and she shared a common desire.

"She wanted my kisses to mean something," he said pointedly. "So I broke off with her."

Geneva stared at him, but he used the mask of darkness to hide from her unspoken queries. Perhaps she'd been naive to think they could lay their cards out on the table, examine their misdirected attraction, and find a way to nip temptation before it grew any bigger. He obviously wasn't being honest with himself, so why did she expect him to admit as much to her? But it didn't stop her from sharing what was on her mind.

"That just-for-fun speech of yours and the phony good-time-guy act are as much a lie as my ex-husband saying he wanted children." She ran a hand through her hair, unwillingly remembering the feel of Wade dragging his big fingers through it as he kissed her.

His hands came down on her shoulders, gripping her as intensely as the expression that covered his face. "You think I'm lying because I'm not telling you what you want to hear. Well, sweetheart, I'll let you in on a little secret."

She wouldn't be surprised if he left fingerprints on her arms, but considering the fierceness of his gaze, she dared not even twitch.

"Most men will pretend to be exactly what you're telling them you want. I'm doing us both a favor by telling you straight up that I'm *not* the one you're looking for." Then, quietly, almost as if he were speaking to himself rather than to her, he added, "I can't love you the way you need to be loved."

Love? Who'd said anything about love? "I never said—"

"And while I have your undivided attention, allow

me to give you a little free advice.'' He drew in a ragged breath before continuing. ''You need to know exactly what it is you want so some smooth-talking conniver doesn't play the bait-and-switch game with you. And, to weed out the pretenders, I suggest you come up with some ways to prove whether they meet your criteria rather than just take their word for it, like you did with your ex.''

With that, he dropped a light kiss on her lips.

''It would be a shame to waste your time on a man who's all wrong for you.''

Geneva pushed the paper plate back on the picnic table and jotted another notation on her list. Wade was right. She needed to be focused if she was to bypass the inappropriate men and quickly move on to better prospects. If she wanted to give birth to enough children to complete a baseball team—which she did—there wasn't much time to waste.

''More potato salad?'' Sean asked in his careful, halting voice.

She regretfully shook her head. ''If I eat another bite I'll burst.''

Jacob bounced at his place on the bench and provided sound effects as he spread his arms to illustrate the explosion.

''Thank you for preparing such a lovely picnic,'' she told her young neighbor. ''You did a wonderful job making the potato salad.''

''And hot dogs,'' Jacob piped in.

Sean pointed a finger at her and rose to start clearing the table. ''I learned from the best.''

Geneva was as proud of him as if he were her own little brother. His willingness to work would see him

far in life. Returning the lid to the pickle jar, she got
up to help him.

"You stay right there," he ordered. "You're my
guest at this picnic." His words were slow and la-
bored. He flashed her a charming grin that reminded
her so much of his older brother's. "Besides, I need
the practice picking up after myself."

She returned his smile at the reference to his house-
keeping. Her gentle admonitions about the clutter in
his house had pricked his pride. Fiercely independent,
he had taken up her challenge and immediately set
about rectifying the problem. It had been less than a
week, but he'd shown no signs of slacking in his new-
found tidiness. Besides, he was too stubborn to allow
himself to be limited by his physical condition. Even
if he did need a little help peeling potatoes.

In that, she knew a common bond with Sean. Just
because her life hadn't gone in the direction she
wanted didn't mean she had to sit back and accept it.
She could, and would, make the most of the good
things that came her way and cut her losses in the
areas that failed to meet her expectations. And that
included time spent in Wade Matteo's company. After
all, he himself had urged her not to waste her time
with someone who was all wrong for her. The first
order of business would be to cancel out of attending
the charity ball with him.

She got up and wiped the evidence of lunch off
Jacob's mouth and hands. By now the pain in her
knee had diminished to a mere twinge.

The table cleared, Sean gave her a friendly salute
and shuffled down the sloping backyard to the water's
edge, where he eased into a lawn recliner and put CD
earphones on his head.

Relaxing in the Sunday-afternoon calm seemed like a good idea, so she went inside for a blanket. When she returned, she spread it under the shade of the dogwood tree and coaxed Jacob to take his nap here. She had just settled down beside him and was watching the pair of birds taking turns delivering meals to their offspring in the door wreath when the low growl of a car engine and the crunch of gravel commanded her attention. Wade was home.

A moment later he was walking her way, his slate-colored slacks hugging his body in a way that drew her eyes to his thick-muscled thighs.

If she was to be successful in her new commitment to maintain focus on her goal, it would be wise to start by eliminating this particular distraction in her life. And it would help if she was standing rather than lying here in a come-hither fashion.

Geneva scrambled to her feet, taking care to soothe her groggy child and urge him to stay put, and met Wade at the picnic table where their voices wouldn't disturb Jacob's nap.

"You didn't have to get up," he told her with a mischievous grin. "I would have been happy to join you on the blanket."

She dropped onto the bench, and he towered over her. "For someone who's so adamant about keeping his distance from women, you sure give a lot of mixed messages."

"Emotional distance," he said, touching his heart. "I never said anything about physical distance."

Geneva was reminded of his earlier comment about not being able to love her the way she needed to be loved. He was right, after all. She needed not just physical love—which she was certain Wade could provide with finesse—but a soul-mate kind of union with a man who matched her on many levels.

To her dismay, he squeezed beside her on the bench and angled his body toward her. His mere closeness served to tie her tongue and stifle her breathing. What had she been about to say to him?

Oh yes. The charity ball.

"About next week…" Against her will, her gaze fixed on the firm slope of his jaw, his powerful neck and the faint shadow that gave evidence of an early-morning shave that was quickly losing the battle against his beard.

"That's what I wanted to tell you. There's no need for you to buy or make new clothes for the ball. If you have a plain black dress, that'll be fine."

"That's not really the problem."

"There's a problem?"

He seemed supremely surprised.

Geneva inched as far away from the intensity of his nearness as the table leg would allow, and twisted the gold necklace that dangled from her neck. "It looks like I won't be going to the charity ball after all." She touched her knee and gave a tiny grimace. "My knee is still hurting a little—" No need going into how little it hurt. "And it looks like dancing is off my list of activities until it's better. Perhaps you should ask someone else now, while you still have time."

"No," he said flatly. The decisiveness of his statement allowed no room for argument. "You should be better by Saturday. If not, we'll skip the dancing. Or just limit ourselves to the slow numbers."

That would be even worse! Standing so close to him, feeling the hard planes and ridges of his body against hers, would only incite her to forget her plans of forever-after with a suitably qualified daddy candidate.

"Wade, you yourself said I shouldn't waste my time on someone I know is all wrong. Don't you remember our talk last night? I'm just like that bride who wanted the kisses she shared to have meaning."

He glared at her, the muscle in his jaw tightening and throbbing. "You're nothing like her. You're independent, and she's clingy. You're—"

The palm of her hand slapped the top of the table. "You know what I'm talking about." She paused, wondering why she was wasting her breath arguing with him. It wasn't as though she needed his approval to ditch their date. But she would like to settle the issue so they could live in neighborly peace. "Why are you doing this to me…to both of us?"

Wade shook his head but didn't look away from her. "I honestly don't know." He hesitated, the confusion clearly evident in his smoky-green gaze. Then, apparently coming to a decision with the turmoil that raged within him, he leaned toward her. His arm touched hers, setting off an involuntary reaction that flared deep to the core of her being. "But I know I like being near you."

Unfortunately, she seconded that opinion.

Putting words aside, he lifted his arm to pull her to him. Foolishly, Geneva didn't resist, not even when he lowered his head to kiss her. Like a lemming rushing to the sea, she allowed him to set the course and followed it mindlessly as he claimed her mouth, stunned her brain…and teased her heart.

When he released her, Geneva could only stare back in mute shock. A few seconds ticked away until

Wade broke the impasse with a brush of his fingers over her cheek and across her lips. Jerking herself back to reality, she clamped her gaping mouth shut. Damn him for having such power over her!

One of the birds darted past them and snagged a winged insect in midair. Watching as it returned to the nest, she knew she had to break the cycle of kisses and frustration that had grown between them. She'd hardly been able to drag herself out of bed for church this morning after a night spent recalling every tiny detail of his every touch, and then tossing in her sleep as her dreams tortured her with visions of where those kisses could have led.

"I want someone..." Her chest ached with the want that he had fostered deep in her soul. "...someone to build a nest with. Someone who'll take an active role in raising his children. *Our* children."

"Don't look at *me*." He moved so he faced straight ahead. Away from her.

"Who said I was looking at you? Besides, you don't fit my criteria." Her misbehaving thoughts reminded her of how well they had fit together each time he'd taken her in his arms.

"Good. I'm relieved. You don't fit my criteria either." A puff of wind threatened to snatch the scrap of paper she'd been writing on earlier, and he stopped it with a well-placed chop from the heel of his hand. "What's this?"

Geneva tried to grab it away from him, but he was too quick. Holding it out of her reach, he squinted to read the penciled notations.

"You're making a husband checklist?"

"Just give it here."

Taking a closer look, he paused and corrected himself. "You're not looking for a husband. You're looking for a babymaker."

He pinned her with his gaze, as if challenging her to argue the fact with him. Certain he wouldn't understand, Geneva opted for silence. Then, as a reluctant afterthought, she declared, "It's what you told me to do."

"One requirement is missing from this list," he said, his voice craggy in its softness. "A man who will love and cherish the kid's mother, and someone the mother can love in return." He let a moment pass before adding, "Someone she can love wholeheartedly. A soul mate."

She squirmed beside him, refusing to deal with the truth he flung at her. Under ideal circumstances, it would be wonderful to find such a quality. But the reality was that life was full of trade-offs. And if she had to choose one over the other, she'd pick a man who would be a good father to her son. And bless them with more children to love. As for husband qualities, she'd be willing to settle for mutual respect and caring concern.

She lifted her chin defiantly. "That's secondary."

Wade responded with a snort of amusement.

"Well, what's your criteria, Mr. Smarty-Pants?" On second thought, maybe she shouldn't have mentioned his pants. Knowing him, he might steer their discussion toward a topic best avoided.

"*If* I ever get married, which is doubtful, it'll be to someone over forty." He absently fingered the small gold Bachelor of the Year pin at his neck. Then, as if strengthened by the reminder of his singleness, he stretched, casually raising his arms over his head and then settled back to face her directly. "To someone who's already finished having all the kids she wants."

Meaning, *certainly not you*. Not that she was interested. Even so, his words stung. Stepping out from the confines of the picnic table, she paced beside the man who instinctively knew how to get under her skin.

"That's ridiculous. From what you say, your heart should get an equal say in whom you marry. But what if you're attracted to someone under forty?" She skidded to a halt. "I'm not talking about me, of course. But, you know, maybe someone *else* under forty?"

Wade got up but didn't bother to approach her. He just stood there and took in what she said without comment. He was making her nervous, and Geneva had an annoying tendency to babble when she was flustered.

"Someone who makes your heart go…flippety-flop," she said, her voice trailing off. She idly swung her arms, then attempting to at least *look* as though she had some small measure of control, perched her hands on her hips.

His gaze followed them, then dragged a slow, purposeful trail up her body and over her face until their eyes met. "I'm attracted to you, but I'm not interested in getting married, and I certainly don't want to have children. So, in this instance, my head has veto power." He casually clapped his palms shut. "Case closed."

Wade rested his hip against the picnic table and took in her combative stance. A small breeze drifted past, rippling her tank top and dancing her dark hair around her shoulders. She had offered him the perfect opportunity to change his mind and back out of taking her to the charity ball. All he had to do was express his genuine concern about the injury to her knee, maybe even offer to do a few chores to keep her off her feet while it healed, and go on his merry way with someone whose career left no room for children in her life. Or, of course, someone over forty who was past the babymaking stage. That would be the easy solution. Certainly the most sane one.

But something told him not to let either of them off the hook that easily. If he were the kind of man to take the easy way out, he would never have risked his family's generations-old farm—not to mention his brother's roots and stability—to turn the place into a country club after his parents died. But he had followed his gut instinct, certain in the knowledge that he'd never rest until he explored this option to the fullest. He had to either succeed at it, or see for himself that it was an impossible venture.

Fortunately for him, the former had come true…in a big way. But in the case of Geneva Jensen, he knew he would have to experience the latter before he could let go and move on.

"Be ready at seven next Saturday," he told her with finality and walked away.

Chapter Six

The restaurant Dr. Grant had suggested turned out to be quite different from the quaint little steak house Geneva had envisioned. And the demure, calf-length dress she'd chosen to wear for the occasion, complete with pearl choker, was all wrong for the setting where they ended up.

Belatedly, Geneva remembered Wade trying to discourage them from going there, and her own insistence that Cassidy's was "perfect." Before Cary had arrived to pick her up, Wade had asked her to take his cell phone "just in case." She had tried to refuse, but he'd insisted, shoving the flip phone into her velvet evening bag.

Patting the booth beside her, she felt for the purse and was comforted by the unfamiliar shape bulging within.

The doctor lifted two grease-spattered menus from behind the jukebox selector at the table and handed her one. No filet mignon or steak tartare here. Their biggest seller seemed to be the "rack o' ribs," judging by its prominent placement on the page and the number of blue-jean-clad customers who'd already ordered the oversize platter that resembled a Conestoga wagon.

The waitress appeared and recited the daily-special choices of barbecue or chicken-fried steak. While the woman waited for them to decide, she scratched the area of abdomen left bare by her midriff T-shirt.

"I'll have the heifer portion of sizzling sirloin, cooked medium well." Even ordering the smallest serving available, Geneva expected to take half of it home with her.

Cary sucked in his lips and released them with a pop. "Give me the homestead helping of ribs and Texas toast."

"Okay," the waitress said, tucking the pencil behind her ear. "But be prepared to wait a while. I got a whole pile of rib orders ahead of yours."

"Then bring me a pitcher of beer while it's cooking. I'm parched."

A moment later, she returned with the beer for him and a glass of ice water for Geneva.

No problem, she thought. The delay in getting their meal would give them more time to get better acquainted. It was already clear they differed in their choices of eating establishments, but that didn't mean they were incompatible in other areas. Perhaps if she got him talking about the children he treated—clearly a subject they did agree upon—she could learn more about him…and decide early whether to invest any more time on future dates with Dr. Cary Grant. Flouting Wade's advice, she went with the direct approach.

"You must really like children to have chosen pediatrics as your field of expertise."

He shrugged and cracked his knuckles. "It's all right if you don't mind having your eardrums pierced by shrill screams or being peed on every day."

"Well, I suppose every job has its drawbacks. What are the parts you *do* like?"

He smiled, and his round cheeks pushed his glasses up on the bridge of his nose. "Having every other Wednesday off to play golf."

The band members chose that moment to strike up a popular country-western tune, and several couples from nearby tables moved to the dance floor.

Cary had to be kidding. At least, she *hoped* so. But she needed to be sure.

Unable to sit still, Wade clicked off the TV and went into the kitchen for ice cream. He wished Geneva had let him baby-sit Jacob instead of taking the boy to his grandmother's for the weekend. At least then Wade would have something to do that would distract him from worrying about his tenant. Geneva had only been gone about thirty minutes, so he really had no reason to worry. Dr. Grant was a ninety-percent-okay fellow. The other ten percent consisted of some minor annoying habits... laughing too loud at his own jokes and occasionally belaboring a subject after others had tried to drop it. No worse than Ellis Tackett's lack of ability to go with the flow.

Instead of going to the freezer, Wade's feet took him to the telephone. He pulled out the phone book, looked up the number and dialed.

"Cassidy's." Music blared in the background and someone near the phone squealed with laughter.

Now that he had them on the line, what did he intend to do? Ask to speak to Geneva? No, she'd never forgive him for interrupting yet another date.

"Yo! You got Cassidy's. What you want?"

Wade gripped the receiver tighter, as if it was his lifeline to Geneva. "I'd like to know if Ms. Geneva Jensen is there."

"Hold on and I'll page her."

"No, don't do that!"

"Look, pal, I don't have time to play games."

"Just tell me if there's a woman there. With a man."

"Yeah, about fifty of 'em. Is that all you wanted? I gotta go unclog a toilet."

"The woman I'm looking for is small, she has thick, curly brown hair, and she's pretty. *Very* pretty."

The man on the other end sighed. *"All* the women in here are small, compared to me, and most of 'em have big hair. As for what she looks like, all I can say is that the more a man has to drink, the prettier a girl is in his eyes. And judging by the guys in here tonight, I'd say all these gals are a ten."

They'd already danced to a couple of fast songs. Geneva was ready to go back to the table, but Cary was intent on keeping her on the dance floor with him. The pace slowed again, and the mellow tones of a tender ballad filled the room. Geneva nodded her head toward their booth, but he ignored her unspoken suggestion. Grabbing her hand, he wrapped himself around her and sang along to the music.

Ooh, you're such a beautiful sight.
Come on, honey, don't put up a fight.
Let me show you my love tonight.
And you'll grow with my love, all right.

Cary was trying his hardest to be romantic, and it showed. His voice was passable, but the words he sang and the manner in which he held her were too much, too soon.

"I'm going to sit down now," she told him.

"Just finish this one song."

Oblivious to her predicament, the lead singer continued the tune, drawing it out with a Southern twang.

Mmm, I want to hold you all night.
Come on, baby, say that you might.
Help me make my future so bright.
Hold me, squeeze me, hug me so tight.

Geneva felt herself growing warm, and it had nothing to do with the romantic feelings the band was trying to encourage. She was annoyed with herself for failing to listen to the tiny voice inside that had whispered, "This isn't the one." Since that had happened at their first meeting, before Cary had even opened his mouth, she'd discounted the feeling, telling herself she was being shallow for judging him on his physical appearance.

She was also a little peeved with Wade for having fixed her up with this guy in the first place. Reluctantly, she decided it wasn't really fair to blame him, though. After all, Cary was probably a nice enough friend to play golf with. How could Wade have known what he would be like on a date?

"I've had enough," she stated in her most firm voice.

Cary blinked at her, as if surprised by her tone, and slowed his swaying until they were barely moving. "You know you want more."

His words were drawled, but not in the Southern style that seemed so exaggerated here. She suspected it had more to do with the beer he'd downed earlier.

"You want lots more. I can tell by the way you're enjoying this song." As the lead singer returned to the chorus, Cary joined in.

Wont' you...
Give me a baby?
Don't you...
Say no or maybe.

Dropping his hands to their former position at the intimate curve below her back, he pulled her to him so they were standing waist to waist and thigh to thigh. If she'd had any doubts before, his intentions were now clearly evident.

"You want kids," he said, stating the obvious. "And I want you. So why wait?"

With that, he plastered his lips on hers.

Wade opened the door to Cassidy's and stepped inside, hoping to catch a glimpse of Geneva having the time of her life. Well, maybe not the time of her life, but at least tolerable.

He stood for a moment, his back to the door, and waited for his eyes to adjust to the smoky haze. So far no sign of her at any of the tables in the serving area of the restaurant. When he found her, he would just watch long enough to know that she was fine and having a good time. And with that accomplished, he could go home with peace of mind.

Or perhaps just sit in the parking lot until he was certain the date was over and she was safely on her way home.

As he rounded the corner, someone clutched at his shirt. Wade hesitated, and that someone slunk closer, wedging herself between him and the dance floor. "Big hair" was a good description for her. Every piece had been stretched out to its full length and starched in place. And the short red dress that clung to every hill and valley looked as if it had been borrowed from a smaller sister. The woman gripped his shirtsleeve and moved her hand up his arm and toward his chest.

"Hey, cutie, wanna dance?"

A movement on the dance floor, a motion that did not fit the rhythm of the music, caught his attention. Looking past the stranger's mound of stiff hair, his gaze fell on a closely entwined couple. The woman was trying without success to pull away from the man. To Wade's consternation, it was the couple he'd been looking for.

Cary seemed not to notice when she drew back her arm in readiness to deliver a well-aimed slap. Her hair came loose from its pearl comb and tumbled in disarray around her small shoulders. Her carefully applied lipstick was smeared, and the overlapped neckline of her dress had skewed to one side.

Wade scowled, furious with himself for allowing things to progress to this point. Setting his hands on the stranger's shoulders, he firmly but gently moved the woman to one side and stormed to the dance floor just as Geneva gave the guy what he deserved.

Now it was Wade's turn.

"Aw, sweetie, you misunderstood," Cary said, holding his jaw in apparent disbelief. "All I was trying to do was show you how I feel about you. Like this."

Despite the fact that a snappy, old-fashioned bluegrass tune had prompted those around them to pour their energy into a breath-taking clog dance, Cary clasped Geneva to him and attempted to repeat his previous offense. Though he was a highly educated doctor, the man obviously could not understand the word *no*. She had just demonstrated the subtle nuances of its definition with a heel grind to his booted foot when suddenly he was jerked away.

His eyes bulging at the unexpected manhandling, Cary stumbled backward, away from Geneva. He lost his footing and was heading south when the strong hands at the nape of his denim shirt yanked him upright, and the aggressor spun him around to face him.

In all her life, Geneva had never seen such a look of fury as Wade wore. His mouth set in rage and determination, he took a firm grip of the front of Cary's shirt, planted his feet, and prepared to pulverize him.

In the space of a second, as her landlord steadied himself for the inevitable punch, Geneva warred between stopping him and cheering him on. Drunk or not, Cary deserved whatever he had coming to him, but considering Wade's tightly coiled stance, she feared his barely withheld anger would explode with that fist-to-jaw contact. Even if Cary had been twice

Wade's size, it wouldn't have been a fair fight, given her rescuer's forceful reaction to what had happened.

Just as Wade was releasing all his power into throwing the punch, Geneva closed her hands around his thick biceps muscle and held on for all she was worth.

"No, don't do it!" she cried.

The action apparently startled him and slowed his strike, but the momentum was already in his thrust, and Geneva was thrown to the floor from the sheer force of it. She landed in a heap, but not before she saw Wade's misdirected blow glance off the side of Cary's face.

Wade paused only a second, and Geneva knew he was tempted to finish the job he'd started. But in the next moment he was bending over her and helping her to her feet.

Ignoring the curious onlookers, he swept his gaze over her as she brushed the dust from her dress. The anguish that distorted his handsome features told her that she looked as bad on the outside as she felt on the inside. He reached out and gently straightened the flap of fabric that folded over her bosom, and that was when she noticed the modesty button dangling by a thread.

"Oh, Gen," was all he said. And when he opened his arms, she stepped willingly into them.

Wade wanted to get her home before the dam burst. He glanced over at Geneva in the passenger seat. An oncoming car's headlights illuminated the tight quiver in her chin and red splotchiness that mottled her face. Considering what she'd been through, she was holding up incredibly well.

"I'm sorry," he said, reaching over to lay a hand on top of her fidgeting fingers. "If I'd known he would be like that, I never would have introduced you."

"It's not your fault." Her voice cracked, and she tried to cover it by clearing her throat. "I was in over my head. I'd never dated much before I married Les, and since then the times have changed."

Wade tightened his grip on her fingers as they passed through the security gate. "Things may have changed some since you last dated, but it's still wrong for a man to bully a woman."

Opening her hand, she laced her fingers with his and tilted her face toward him. "If you hadn't been there, I don't know what I would have..."

Her voice trailed off, and a lone tear trickled down her cheek. They were almost home, but he couldn't just take her back to the house where she would retreat alone to the apartment and close the door that would separate them not only physically but emotionally. She needed to be with someone...someone who cared for her and would help her forget the night's events...or help her put them in the proper perspective.

Instead of choosing the right fork that would take them to the house, he veered left and went past the clubhouse. Then driving past the groundskeeper's shack, he took the maintenance path to the back nine and cut across the green at the sixteenth hole.

"Wade, what are you doing? You're going to ruin the golf course."

She was right. The ground was still soft from an afternoon shower, but a couple of ruts in the course were minor compared to what she'd been through.

"It's easily fixed," he said. A lot easier, in fact, than fixing her shattered spirit. He pulled up beside a gnarled oak whose trunk split in two at shoulder height, and he got out to retrieve a blanket from the car. "I thought you might want to sit under the stars and settle your nerves before we go back to the house."

She eyed him and the blanket warily and made no move to get out of the car.

"It's okay," he assured her, holding the faded fabric away from him in a gesture of innocence. "The blanket is to protect your skirt." He motioned toward a wooded path. "When I was a kid I came here whenever I needed to get away from my problems."

She hesitated a moment longer, but eventually joined him as he led the way to a clearing beside a small stream. He spread the blanket in a patch of moonlight and waited for her to settle onto it before he seated himself beside her. He folded his arms over his knees.

Geneva watched him a long moment, wondering briefly if he had ulterior motives for bringing her here. Almost instantly, she rejected that thought. Cary had been insensitive and manipulative, but Wade was the opposite. In the short time she'd known him, she'd come to realize he was an honest and direct man. If he wanted to seduce a woman, he had no need for trickery or subterfuge. And she was certain there were enough willing women waiting in the wings that he had no need to pursue a homebody such as herself.

Wade reached over and picked up a green twig that had fallen from a tree and proceeded to strip the bark from it while he waited for his secret sanctuary to work its magic on Geneva. It wasn't long before she was lying back on the blanket and staring up at the stars that were nearly obliterated by the bright glow of the moon.

"I'm really sorry about tonight," he told her once again. "I had no idea Cary would be such a jerk."

Guilt bit at him as he acknowledged to himself that he knew ahead of time the date he'd fixed her up with might not work out. But he hadn't wanted Geneva to be hurt either.

"I'm not mad at you for what he did." Her voice was soft and relaxed now, the tightness gone from her tone and features. "I'm not even mad that you followed us to Cassidy's. I hate to think what might have happened if you hadn't been there."

Wade's stomach tightened at the thought. It would have been all his fault if events had continued in the way they were heading. He hated to think what might have happened if he had been delayed by as little as five minutes.

A companionable silence reigned for the next few minutes. Wade lay back onto the blanket beside her and pointed up beyond the treetop. "When I was a kid I'd watch the bats dive and swoop for insects."

Geneva squinted toward where he'd pointed and was soon rewarded with the sight of a bat ballet, complete with dizzying spins and graceful midair loops. "Did anyone else know about this place?"

Such a long moment passed that she thought he might not answer.

He put his hands behind his head, his elbow barely grazing her shoulder. "You're the first one I've ever brought here," he admitted. "Sean knew about the place, but he couldn't navigate the trail."

Although he didn't say so, she suspected that was

why he came here…so he could spend a little time away from his younger brother. "Yes, I suppose his crutches would slow him down."

Wade shook his head. "He was in a wheelchair most of the first ten years of his life. The doctors all said he'd never walk, and my parents believed them."

He sighed, remembering the frustration of that life-changing time. For several years he'd lifted his brother out of the wheelchair and encouraged him to stand as long as possible to strengthen the muscles in his legs. When the boy was finally able to stand unassisted for several seconds, Wade felt certain he would eventually be able to walk. Fortunately, he and his brother shared the common trait of stubborn determination.

"I got it into my head one summer that he would walk onto the schoolbus when school started again in the fall."

Geneva turned toward him and smiled. "And it worked!"

"Not exactly. My mother thought I was setting him up for failure and disappointment, so she tried to make us stop."

"What? How could a mother—"

Wade touched a finger to her lips to silence her protest. "It's not what you think. Many kids born with Joubert syndrome never walk or get a mainstream education. The doctor painted a rather grim picture, leading my parents to believe Sean might not even make it to adulthood. But I had a feeling he could eventually walk, and Sean and I were determined to prove the doctor wrong. It just took a year longer than I had planned."

Geneva did a quick mental calculation and realized

that Sean had graduated from wheelchair to crutches about the time Wade graduated from college. The image of him steadfastly helping his brother exercise and practice day after day was at odds with the fun-and-games party boy and womanizer she'd thought him to be.

"Not everyone would devote himself so thoroughly to helping someone else." She hadn't meant to voice the thought, and Wade seemed to want to change the subject. But that didn't stop her from telling him what she thought of his unselfishness. "Your brother is very fortunate to have you in his corner," she said, laying a hand on his arm.

He looked down at her hand but made no move to touch her. "I look after the people I care about."

An irrational sense of disappointment crept over her when he seemingly ignored the plea for closeness that her touch conveyed, but his words had closed the distance between them.

"You came to Cassidy's." She knew why. She needed to hear him say it. "You were looking for me?"

He nodded and lifted a hand to her hair. As he pushed the heavy locks behind her shoulder and drew the backs of his fingers across her cheek, moonlight spilled through the leaves and fell onto his face, showing Geneva a desire that mirrored her own. "Yes," he said in answer to her question. "I came looking for you. Because I care about you."

She could tell it took a lot for him to admit that last part. A whole minute, maybe two, ticked by as the meaning penetrated her brain, and especially her heart. Geneva turned her face toward his touch, her lips grazing his hand and her soul crying out for him to show her with his hands, his lips, even his body how much he cared.

Wade froze, stilling the mindless caress he'd started. But the hesitation was only momentary. In the next instant she was in his arms. It felt so right. If heaven was anything like this, then he vowed to get right with God so he could spend an eternity savoring the pleasure that came from holding the woman of his dreams.

She leaned back on the blanket, her hair flowing around her like water through the creek bed. Her expression—soft, welcoming and giving—beckoned him, and the trickling of the creek seemed to urge him on. "I care about you, too," she told him.

He bent to kiss her, and as he did so, the button at her bosom released its tentative hold, revealing soft, pearly skin. Wade reached for the fold of black cloth to pull it closed, but she pressed his hand to her heart. He paused, knowing that the rapid staccato matched the desperate beat of his own heart. And, for the first time, he admitted to himself that he was glad the other dates hadn't worked out. In fact, he'd known when he set them up that they weren't exactly right for Geneva. Though their surface qualities had matched what she was looking for, he'd intuitively known she wouldn't click with either of them on a deeper, more personal level. Guilt stabbed at him as he thought of the predicament he'd put her in tonight. "I'm sorry that Cary turned out to be such a jerk," he repeated.

"I don't blame you," she said, lifting her face to his.

He took it as an invitation and kissed her again, this time with such feeling that it left both of them breathless. Her heart pounded harder, and he sought to quiet it by covering his palm over her bare skin. She drew in a quick breath, and the fabric fell away, exposing two softly rounded breasts barely confined within a thin scrap of lace. With an impatience he'd never known before, he released the front clasp, freeing them to burn beneath his hungry perusal. She was the most beautiful woman he'd ever seen—the sweetest and most loving—and his body responded accordingly.

She had felt his physical reaction to her—there was no way he could hide it—and she shyly unbuttoned his shirt. A cool summer breeze wafted between them, bringing the soft orbs of her skin to pert, pink peaks.

Wade grew light-headed at the sight, but a quick intake of air steadied him enough to rip the remaining buttons off his shirt. Then he unfastened the belt at her small waist and flung aside the wraparound folds of her dress.

Thankful the clouds that had brought the afternoon showers had passed, he drank in the sight of her moonlight-splashed body. Her eyes seemed to gleam in anticipation as he covered her body with his own. He took her mouth, savoring the taste and feel of her lips as he allowed his hands to trace the path his gaze had forged earlier, starting with the full swell of her breasts, first cupping them in his hands and teasing the tips to hard eager knots, and then trailing down to her belly and below.

Her arms slid around his neck, and he rested his weight on her, their bare upper bodies abrading in a sensuous sliding of skin on skin.

Wade reached down to remove his belt lest it scratch her, and as his hand brushed her abdomen, he thought he felt an imperfection on the delicate skin that teased him and tortured his senses. A scar, perhaps? Shifting to one side, one leg still draped across her thighs, he again ran his hand over her belly, feeling more clearly the soft, silky ridges.

She pulled at his neck, urging him back to the closeness they'd shared a mere moment before. But Wade needed to see her, see all of her. He wanted to feast on every aspect of her, even if it was an appendectomy scar or the lingering trace of a bicycle wreck. His finger dipped into the shallow indentation, marking the spot as the moon waxed full and spotlighted the faint silvery ribbons that laced her belly.

Wade drew back. These were no surgery scars, nor were they evidence of a childhood mishap. His alarm must have shown, for Geneva sat up and pulled the dress to her.

"What's wrong."

"Stretch marks," he said, still assimilating the meaning behind them. "You have stretch marks."

She tilted her head, obviously confused by his sudden change of attitude. "Yes. They come from having a baby."

Wade nodded. "That's what I thought." And babies meant commitment, parenting, and most of all risk.

It was a risk he couldn't take...not only for himself, but for Geneva and the new life that might result from their union. He carried no protection with him, but even if he had, a thin bit of latex was not enough to assure him he would remain child-free after their encounter, blissful as it was certain to be. The risk just wasn't worth it.

"We can't do this," he said, rising to his feet and pulling on his buttonless shirt. Geneva looked hurt and embarrassed. Although he felt like kicking himself for hurting her even after protecting her from Cary, Wade knew he couldn't soften now. Better that she suffer a little hurt tonight than a much greater pain in the future.

"It's just not worth it," he said with conviction.

Chapter Seven

It was at times like these that Geneva wondered why she bothered to take her promises so seriously. After the brush-off Wade had given her last night, it just wasn't worth it.

But here she was, an honor-bound idiot, sipping champagne while the upper crust of Kinnon Falls inspected Wade's latest arm adornment…her. She was beginning to wish she hadn't promised her mother that Jacob could stay all weekend. At least then she could have used picking up her son as an excuse to leave the charity gala early.

Considering the fact that she'd foolishly cried herself to sleep last night—not because of the incident with Cary, but because she'd felt so stupid for throwing herself at and being rejected by the town playboy—she was glad she hadn't spent more time making the dress she now wore. With **all** the bad feelings clinging to it, she doubted she'd wear it again.

But the simplicity of the pattern and ease of sewing

it did nothing to diminish its overall effect. The shimmery jacquard print, with ivy leaves curling around itself, caressed her figure, and the aqua color made her eyes lighten to a pale caramel.

Ignoring Wade's darkly handsome gaze, she resisted the urge to knock back the rest of the champagne and contented herself instead with studying the throng of people that milled around them in the hotel ballroom. Some of the faces were familiar to her, as she had previously seen them at the country club. There were the chief of police, some local television celebrities, high-powered business executives and even a couple of semi-pro athletes. And one woman so pregnant it looked as though she might give birth at any minute. Fortunately for the expectant woman, several prominent physicians were also in attendance, which wasn't surprising, given the fact that the recipient of this fund-raiser ball was the nearby children's hospital.

With an election coming up in a few months, several local political notables had also deemed it prudent to attend this gathering of high-profile people. And they all seemed to know Wade personally. Especially the women.

Moving along the edge of the crowd, a newspaper photographer swept the room with his lens.

The band opened with a lively rock tune, prompting Geneva to tap her toe in rhythm to the primal beat. Wade touched her arm, and Geneva gave herself a mental scolding for allowing herself a thrill at the simple gesture.

"Dance?"

She hesitated long enough for him to notice. It would be torture to step into the arms of the man who wanted her for no other reason than to ward off aggressive females. Well, she wouldn't be one of those pathetic women, rolling out her emotions like a welcome mat, only to have him tread all over them. She'd dance with him, but only a few sets, and when enough time had passed and her promise was adequately fulfilled, she'd claim a headache and ask to be taken home. It wouldn't be a lie either. Just standing close to him, taking in his faint male scent, hearing the soothing rumble of his voice, and filling her eyes with the eloquent figure he cut in his tuxedo made her head—and heart—pound.

"You don't have to worry," he said, holding out his hand. His voice was low and assuring. "This isn't Cassidy's, and I'm not Cary."

Her reply was gentle, betraying the emotions she tried to hide. "No, you're not." But the thought did little to comfort her. Although she harbored no fear he would repeat the other man's obnoxious behavior, she had more reason to be wary of Wade. For it was he who held her heart in his hands. And if she didn't proceed cautiously, she would risk having it crushed.

Gingerly, she went to him. But despite her initial hesitation, she soon found herself falling into step with him, swinging and twirling with abandon. And she liked it.

She liked the way her escort looked at her even more, his gaze possessive and hungry, and his arms warm and welcoming.

The spell was cracked a little while later when he noticed her quiet reflection.

"Thinking about me?" A small dimple creased his tanned cheek.

Indirectly. Why did it seem as though all thoughts

led back to Wade? "I was thinking about a house I saw for sale on the way over here."

"The one on Kagle Avenue?"

"That's the one. It looks like it would be a great place to raise Jacob." She sighed, letting herself lean into his arms as the gentle strains of "Midnight Paradise" swept over them. "I wish I could afford to buy it now."

She felt him stiffen slightly, and she supposed he was concerned that she'd leave him with no one to help watch out for his brother.

"It won't happen soon." On the surface, her comment was a simple reassurance to Wade that she'd be around for a while. But beneath it was the unsettling realization that she didn't want to leave his house. Not just yet. Though she'd only been there a short time, it already felt like home, like she and Jacob belonged there.

"Not if I can help it." Wade bent his head close to hers, and a surge of hope welled within her when it seemed as though he might kiss her.

She was enjoying this too much. Enjoying the feel of his strong arms around her, the undivided attention he bestowed on her. Although her head understood that charm was a skill of Wade's, a skill he had used with unerring success on dozens, maybe even scores, of women, her heart compelled her to lift her face toward him.

It was as if instinct took over after that, binding them together in an intimate dance that mated lips and souls and made her wish for things that were best avoided. His hand slid to the small of her back, and as he guided her closer, she became aware that he wanted the same.

He kissed her—gentle, sweet and ever so patient—but it wasn't enough. When she opened her eyes, she found him watching her with heavy-lidded green eyes that seemed to peer directly into her heart.

A movement nearby distracted him, and she followed his gaze to the pregnant woman they'd seen earlier. Although the stranger was dancing with someone, her curiosity was evident, and she made no effort to hide the fact that she was staring.

Wade guided Geneva into the shadows. "Better?"

"Yes, much." Hidden in the darker recesses of the room, she felt as though she had him more to herself. Back here, there was no need to share him with curious onlookers.

At her affirmative nod, he added, "I thought you'd want to keep a low profile. Wouldn't want to scare off a potential husband, being seen with me."

Although he'd said it jokingly, his words were tinged with a painful truth.

"Wade, that's not what I meant." Perhaps she might have felt that way a few days ago, but now, well, something had changed between them. Something had happened last night that made her see him in a different light. And the new perspective both thrilled and frightened her. Suddenly her reputation no longer seemed an issue. More important was being in the company of the man who made her forget her ordinariness and made her feel sexy, exotic and desirable. The plan had been to get through this evening as uneventfully as possible and return home at the first opportunity, but in truth she wanted to stay right here with him. To spend the evening dancing with Wade Matteo, smug in the knowledge that most of the other women at the ball envied her. It was reckless, that much was certain, but her heart had a mind of its own. "You're the one I want to—"

The spotlight that had been bouncing among the crowd fell on them and lingered as if the entire room were waiting for her to finish what she'd been about to say. A flashbulb went off, letting her know that what had started as their semiprivate moment was now captured on film. Self-conscious now, Geneva grew silent and peered through the harsh light at Wade.

He seemed unruffled by the attention, moving her effortlessly through the dance, their steps in attunement even though their lifestyles were not. "Just try to ignore it," he urged as the ball of light encircled them in a public caress. "After a while, you won't even notice it."

How could she ignore such a blatant intrusion? It didn't seem to bother Wade at all. Perhaps, as he'd suggested, he had grown used to such attention. As a prominent businessman and avowed ladies' man, he had become accustomed to living in the limelight. He was no stranger to having his face grace the society page of the Kinnon Falls newspaper and being recognized in public as the Bachelor of the Year.

Geneva missed a step and came down heavily on the top of his Italian-leather shoes. "I'm sorry," she said, grateful for the steadying arm he wrapped around her. "The light is blinding me."

Though she'd reluctantly acknowledged, to herself if not to Wade, her feelings for him, this came as a timely reminder of just how different they were. Whereas her idea of true happiness was to be at home, quietly spending time with her family, he actually seemed to relish being in the public spotlight. She would never want to live like this. Not that it would have made any difference…he'd made it clear he wasn't interested in a relationship with her. But, unfortunately, that didn't stop her from wanting him.

Another camera bulb flashed, and stars floated in front of her eyes.

Wade turned them both so the photographer could get a good shot and gave a brilliant smile. Maybe if the journalist got what he wanted, he'd leave them alone and move on to another subject.

But when he looked back down at the woman in his arms, he saw that she looked not only dazzling, but dazzled. Her eyes were glazed, and she seemed to have a hard time focusing.

She was clearly out of her element, but she was making a noble effort to be gracious despite the unwelcome scrutiny. She hadn't wanted to come with him tonight and had merely done so, he supposed, out of obligation. He was glad she had come. That made him nervous. As did the fact that he wanted to protect her from the stares and whispers that reverberated around them.

The song came to an end and the band struck up another fast number, fortuitously granting him the opening he'd wanted to get them off the dance floor. He looped an arm around her waist and started to lead her to the table. "Are you ready to leave now?"

She stepped back and clutched his elbow as he guided her through the crowd, but he was abruptly cut off by the blonde in the designer-label maternity dress. At his sudden stop, Geneva collided into the back of him. As her hands fell on his waist, she was once again acutely aware of the raw power that his well-tailored suit could not conceal.

"I win the bet," the woman declared. "Deanna didn't think you'd come, but I told her you never miss these galas."

Wade reached over and laid a hand atop Geneva's. "Hello, Renee." The words seemed to roll off automatically as he attempted to maneuver past her, keeping his body wedged conveniently between them. Unfortunately, this Renee person turned aside and purposely blocked his path with her distended belly.

"Who's that? The latest in your long line of—"

"Good to see you again," he hastily interjected. Wade seemed clearly agitated in the woman's presence, and it was obvious he was trying to avoid her. And maybe avoid introducing them? He backed up to pursue an alternate route of escape, but Geneva's curiosity had been piqued.

She reached past him and extended her free hand. "Hi, I'm Geneva Jensen."

"Renee Austin." She leaned forward and shook his date's hand. "Let me warn you...if you have your sights set on *this* man," she said, congenially hitching a thumb toward Wade, "you may as well forget it." She smiled and casually spread her fingers over her abdomen. "He's only after one thing, and once he gets it he moves on to the next person on his list."

Geneva had heard a similar caution before. From the offhand way in which the other woman told this, she could have been a supermarket shopper cautioning Geneva to avoid the lighter grapefruits and choose the more substantial ones instead. Renee followed her statement with a gusty laugh, and Geneva saw the panic that filled Wade's eyes.

"Careful," he said, forcing a laugh. "You'll tarnish my reputation."

He pretended to be inordinately concerned that they might be blocking the dance floor, and when Geneva started to suggest to Renee that they go someplace quieter to chat, he quickly interrupted by pulling her to him and "reminding" her of their other plans... plans about which she'd known nothing until now.

"Sweetheart, at another time that would be fun," he said, pulling at his tie and addressing the second half of his statement to Renee, "but I was counting on that candlelight wine-and-cheese party she promised me."

It was hard to tell exactly what he'd said, what with the music blaring around them. "Party?"

Laying a hand intimately aside her neck, he gave her a beseeching look. "You can't have forgotten already? That party for two? On a blanket under the stars?"

Geneva stopped breathing as he casually lifted her hair from her shoulder, then trailed a finger down her collarbone. The memory of their closeness last night flooded her, and despite the fact that they were in a room with at least a couple hundred other people her body responded as if they were once again alone by the brook. The breath she'd been holding came out as a wistful sigh.

"Still at your old games, huh, Wade?" Renee said with a meaningful wink. Then she turned to Geneva. "It was nice meeting you. Remember what I said— don't lose your heart to this guy. He's not the type to settle down with one person." At that, she gave a little wave and returned to her companion.

The woman's words were a bucket of cold water that drenched her soul. What had she been thinking?

What was the matter with her, falling for a man like Wade…a man who was the complete opposite of all that she sought? Well, maybe not *complete* opposite. He did, after all, have a body to die for and the most gorgeous face she'd ever seen. But lean, hard muscles and skilled hands and lips were not necessarily qualities she was looking for. As for that face, she had only to remind herself of his skill at using those penetrating green eyes to charm women into giving him what he desired. And, as proven by Renee, they were so enthralled by him they were incapable of holding a grudge even after he'd dumped them and moved on to the next name on his list.

Though neither had said as much, Geneva was certain the child was Wade's. Why else would he have been so anxious to get away from Renee, and prevent them from talking? From comparing notes. It sure seemed obvious that he wanted nothing to do with the baby. Oddly enough, Renee seemed satisfied with the way things were between them. Oh, what power the charmer possessed!

Well, he wasn't going to charm her. Geneva wanted nothing to do with a love-'em-and-leave-'em kind of man. Pulling away from his mesmerizing touch, she made her way back to the table and picked up her velvet bolero jacket. And all the while, she tried unsuccessfully to wipe away the image of his questioning gaze…his seemingly sincere confusion over her abrupt departure.

He reached her as she slid her arm into one velvet sleeve. Holding the jacket for her as she finished pulling it on, he made no further move to touch her. Nor did he say anything else about their supposed candlelight party. In fact, he was the perfect gentleman. The stark contrast between his behavior toward her in front of Renee and the way he acted now served as a painful reminder that he wanted nothing to do with a woman like herself. He wanted no part of a woman with ideas of permanence and togetherness and eternal devotion.

A woman with stretch marks.

She gathered the jacket protectively around her shoulders and turned away from him.

"Geneva? Is something wrong?"

There was no justification for her being so annoyed with Wade. He'd made it clear right from the start that he didn't want a relationship with her. More importantly, she didn't want a relationship with *him*. And she'd known all along that he only wanted her to accompany him to this ball to help ward off unwanted female attention...as he'd accomplished with Renee.

He'd used her tonight. But it could have been worse. He could have used her as he had Renee. And if it hadn't been for the stretch marks, she might have found herself in the same situation.

"No, nothing's wrong." Nothing that wouldn't be solved when the birds on her door wreath were old enough to fly away. Once that happened, she would close the door between their residences and padlock it shut. "I am curious about one thing, though."

They walked together toward the patio. From there they would follow the brick path to the parking lot and head home. But not before she got her question answered.

"Is she the first girl you've gotten pregnant?"

It was none of her business, and Renee had seemed unconcerned that the father of her child had no interest in stepping forward to claim his responsibility. It was the baby Geneva worried about. No child should have to grow up without a father, especially not when the only thing keeping the father away was an appalling lack of duty and honor.

"What are you talking about?"

As they paused near the door, a waiter excused himself and moved past them, carrying a tray of hot hors d'oeuvres.

"You don't need to play coy with me. It doesn't take a hired detective to figure out what happened between you two."

He pulled open the door, clearly intent on ending this unwanted discussion. "You have a vivid imagination. Have you ever considered writing mystery novels?"

Still holding the door, he gestured for her to go before him. But Geneva wasn't so easily put off. It wasn't necessary for her to know the answer, but a morbid curiosity, and maybe a desire to prove him a scoundrel, which would quell her fascination for him, compelled her to press on. With any luck, his response would help break the tentative bonds that had grown between them and allow her to get on with her life.

She needed to close her heart to Wade so she could open it to someone better suited to her goals and needs.

"You didn't answer my question."

At about that time, an attractive man in his thirties stepped inside. As he passed between them, he hesitated. After a brief pause, he turned to Wade and laughed. "Still keeping them in the dark, eh, Matteo?"

The two men greeted each other with hearty handshakes and good-natured slaps on the back. "Dan, you ol' son of a gun! Where've you been these past few years?"

"In Tennessee, working at my uncle's electronics firm." They released each other and stepped apart. "I came home to visit my family and heard you were hosting another fund-raiser bash. What's this about you not offering yourself for the bachelor auction this year? That's a *tradition*."

Geneva cleared her throat. She wasn't up to hearing boisterous retellings of the good old days.

Wade remembered his manners and drew her into their circle. "Daniel Etheridge, I'd like you to meet my, uh...*neighbor*, Geneva Jensen."

She noticed he didn't refer to her as his "friend." Doing so might have led others to think she was his *girl*friend. Except for that brief moment while they were dancing, he seemed hell-bent on pushing her away. Okay, so she had stretch marks. Surely there were more valid reasons for disclaiming her as a love interest.

Then a disquieting possibility dawned on her. Oh no, he couldn't! Not again.

Dan smiled down at her. "Excuse me a moment while I grab one of those shrimp rolls."

"What's with you?" Wade asked after his friend had gone. "You look like the gopher that swallowed the golf ball."

"You're not going to do it to me again. Not if I have anything to say about it."

She edged toward the door, desperate to escape from more torture. Although she'd wanted to harden her heart to Wade so she could be open to meeting more suitable men, she had no desire to undergo yet another ill-fated matchup.

"You know what they say about three strikes and you're out. Well, I'm out of here."

Wade grabbed her wrist as Dan turned toward them, his paper napkin filled with fried snacks. There was no way she could wrench free of Wade's iron-hard grasp without making a scene. She might be physically trapped, but that didn't mean she had to go along with his latest scheme to rid himself of her.

"What made you want to leave all of a sudden?" Wade asked in all innocence.

"You! Or, more specifically, that matchmaking gleam in your eyes." She drew in a deep breath, and was oddly satisfied when he noticed her jacket part with the movement. "I'm quite capable of finding a man on my own, without any help from a man who sells himself at bachelor auctions."

"Hey, I only did that a couple of times. Maybe seven." He maintained his grip on her wrist. "Besides, you'll never find a guy more perfect than Dan. I'd trust him with my own sister...if I had a sister."

"Sure, that's what you said the last two times." She tried to break free, but quit struggling when the gold clasp on her watch bit into her wrist.

"Dan is everything you're looking for in a man," Wade informed her. "He's working his way up the corporate ladder, he's reliable, he's a family kind of guy and...and...completely unspontaneous."

Geneva blinked, trying to follow his logic on that last trait.

"He's the complete opposite of me," Wade continued, as if that was all it took to satisfy her needs.

"You also told me Ellis and Cary were the perfect

guys for me." Unnecessarily, she added, "Neither of them worked out."

"Dan's different. I grew up with him. We were best friends all the way through college, until he moved away."

"Shrimp curl?" Dan thrust his napkin toward them as he rejoined the group. His gaze dropped to Geneva's wrist, which Wade still clasped.

"No thanks." Wade lifted her arm and made a show of fumbling with the clasp on her watch. "There, I think that should keep it from coming loose again."

Then, with a smug smile at having explained away their contact, he dropped her arm and moved to one side so she and Dan were standing beside each other.

At that moment, Renee went past them on the arm of an attractive gentleman and paused briefly to introduce them to her husband. Geneva's gaze automatically dropped to the other woman's ring finger. Sure enough, it was graced with a beautiful gold band and enormous diamond ring.

As the couple moved to resume their trek across the room, Renee leaned closer, lifted her eyebrow toward Dan, and whispered to Geneva, "Smart move. You're much better off with this one."

She was gone before Geneva could respond.

Relentless, Wade was determined to draw the subject back to his matchmaking. "I was just telling Geneva that you and I were college roommates."

Dan laughed. "Talk about complete opposites," he said, parroting Wade's earlier description. "I think it was Wade's mission in life to corrupt me. And all along I was trying to set a good example to reform him. Neither of us was successful."

Grinning in response to the affectionate slur on his character, Wade threw her an "I told you so" glance.

Geneva narrowed her eyes at the man who had managed to turn her emotions upside down lately. Something didn't make sense. She had always instinctively steered herself away from carousers and flirts, preferring men of stability and permanence, yet something had drawn her to Wade. Something that made her feel as though they connected on some deeper level, and that they both shared common desires. But all signs—and Wade's own admissions—indicated he was exactly the kind of man she needed to avoid. It was almost as if he were two separate people. As if there was one face he showed to the public and another, one she'd seen mere glimpses of, when they were alone together.

Cautioning herself not to pursue that line of thought any further, she returned her attention to their conversation. By now, Wade had steered the discussion to the latest mystery thriller coming to the local movie cinema.

"I've been wanting to see that one," Dan said.

"Really?" Was it her imagination, or did Wade actually rub his palms together? "Then why don't you take Geneva? She loves scary movies."

"How did you know?" She'd never told him about her passion for intrigue and suspense. Most people, left to guess according to her personality, would assume she favored quiet, serious dramas.

"There was never a question," Wade replied with a wink. He whacked Dan on the shoulder. "What do you say?"

"Well, uh…" Dan looked to her as if to see what

she thought of Wade's unexpected suggestion. "Do you want to?"

Geneva sighed. Not so much about the latest matchmaking effort, but for what might have been. She needed to get herself off that hopeless carousel and look to some prospects that were actually promising. Still, she let her eyes meet Wade's, silently questioning him to see if this was what he really wanted.

She didn't know what she expected to see there, but she couldn't help being disappointed when he raised his eyebrows and gave her a nod that said, *Go ahead…what are you waiting for?*

He was right. What *was* she waiting for…Prince Charming on a white stallion? The only horses around here were those at the club's stables, and she didn't recall seeing any white animals among them. As for Dan Etheridge, who knew? He just might be the one for her.

She'd grown closer—dangerously close—to Wade, especially after their time by the creek last night. He was a hazard to her heart, just as an electrical outlet was a hazard to her son's exploring fingers. Whenever Jacob was headed for danger, she distracted him from his folly by offering him something more suitable to play with. Perhaps Dan would be a safe distraction for her…and make her forget her folly of falling in love with Wade.

"Sure," she said, forcing a tone of interest. "That sounds like fun."

"Great!" Wade clapped his hands together as if a deal had just been sealed. "Perfect. This is just perfect!"

Dan seemed nice enough. And the shallow side of her appreciated his handsome face and athletic build.

It stung to be brushed off like unwanted lint, but perhaps it was better this way. Maybe Wade was right. Maybe Dan was the perfect guy.

If that was the case, why did she feel as if this match was so wrong?

Chapter Eight

It was the right thing to do. Get her off the market so he'd stop thinking about her, and do his best friend a favor at the same time. A *huge* favor.

Wade stood at the side yard, debating whether to say something to her. And if so, what? Perhaps he could give her a little pep talk. His last two fix-ups hadn't been successful, and he suspected she was going into this evening's date with the wrong attitude.

Geneva shook out a yellow shirt that was barely bigger than her hand and hung it on the line strung across the back of the yard. Wade crossed the grass and reached into her laundry basket for a pale green child's shirt. Handing it to her, he said, "You can use the dryer in the utility room anytime you want."

She smiled, but it didn't reach her eyes. She was obviously still miffed with him about wrangling yet another date for her last night. He was just glad that she had accepted the arrangement despite her irritation with him.

"Thanks, but I prefer to hang Jacob's clothes outside so the sun can brighten them. Besides, it makes them smell fresher." She started to say something else, then appeared to think better of it. Instead, she took the tiny blue jeans that he held out to her and pinned them to the line.

Wade thought about the fresh smell that always accompanied her. Leaning closer, he thought he caught a hint of lemon. An irrational urge swept over him to nuzzle her neck and enjoy the warm, clean scent of her. But then his highly developed sense of self-preservation kicked in, and he changed the subject to one that was guaranteed to put some healthy distance between them.

"Are you all ready for your date with Dan this evening?" Taking in the thigh-revealing shorts and body-hugging tank top she wore, he hoped not. Maybe she should change into an ankle-length dress made of burlap.

No, wait, that wasn't the right attitude. He should be hoping Geneva would knock Dan off his feet, inspire a whirlwind engagement, and then move to Tennessee to have a dozen more kids with him. Then everyone would be happy.

Well, not everyone. Sean would hate to see her go. He was turning into quite the chef under her tutelage, and his apartment was staying reasonably neat, too. And, well, Wade supposed he'd miss her, too. And the little rug rat.

But that was all the more reason to ensure the success of this latest matchup. If she and Jacob were happy, and his best friend was happy, then he'd be thrilled. Mostly.

A little.

Okay, he'd be satisfied he did the right thing by fixing her up with a man who could give her what she needed. Who could give her what *he* couldn't.

"Dan won't be here for another couple of hours," she said in answer to his question.

"Do you want me to baby-sit?" At her skeptical glance, he added, "Sean can help."

"Thanks, but that's not necessary. Jacob will stay at my mother's until after the movie." The laundry basket was almost empty now, and she'd started hanging up socks. "The eggs have all hatched. It won't be long before the baby birds fly away."

Wade nodded. "I suppose that'll be a help in your dating life. Of course, it would be a moot point if you and Dan should decide to get married."

Geneva picked up the basket and tucked it under one arm while directing a soul-searching gaze straight at him.

Maybe he shouldn't have said that last part out loud. It probably was rushing things a tad, after all.

"Why are you working so hard to push me away?"

"What?" he said, feigning innocence.

She had a death grip on the laundry basket. "Something passed between us the other night, and no matter how much you try to deny it, it's still going to be there."

Wade felt his shoulders sag. He had hoped she wouldn't see the thing that had scared him so profoundly. Hoped they could pretend it had never happened. But she was a perceptive and honest woman. She would need to close things between them before she could move on to someone else. To the right man for her. To Dan.

And, to allow her to move her life in a direction that would bring her the happiness she deserved, he would have to convince her—convince them both—that they were wrong for each other.

Taking the basket from her, he led her to the picnic bench. When she sat down, curiosity apparent in her eyes, he joined her and placed the basket on the ground beside them.

"When I was a little boy, I developed a terrible allergy to strawberries. Every time I ate them, I got a rash on my chest and stomach, but I didn't want to give them up."

She frowned.

"The point is, strawberries and I weren't meant to be. No matter how much I liked them, there could be serious complications if I didn't stay away from them." He placed a hand on her wrist. "In a similar way, you and I are wrong for each other."

Geneva pulled her arm away from him. "So you're saying I'm like a rash to you?"

"No, that's not what I'm saying at all." She wasn't making this easy. He couldn't blame her. After all, he hadn't exactly been standoffish toward her the other night. Or even on occasion before that. "It's just that when you and I were on the blanket by the creek—"

"My stretch marks reminded you of your aversion to strawberries," she supplied for him.

He sat still for a long moment. With other women, it had been simpler to don the act of a player...a man who refused to settle down with one woman. There were fewer questions and fewer *tsk-tsks* that way. But he couldn't continue doing that with Geneva. He owed her an explanation. He owed her the truth.

Softly, hoping beyond hope that she would understand his reasoning and not press him to change his mind, he said, "Your stretch marks reminded me that I don't want kids."

She flinched as if he'd struck her. "You don't want Jacob," she said, her voice flat.

"Jake's a terrific kid," he countered. "I'd be proud if he were my son."

Geneva gripped the edge of the picnic table until her knuckles whitened. "You're not making sense."

It looked as though the truth alone wouldn't be enough. He'd have to give her the full story...one which he'd started when they were alone together the other night.

One which would allow her to go on her date this evening with an open mind and a heart that was receptive to all the good that Dan had to offer. He would lose her to another man, and he hoped that man would be Dan. His friend would treat her well and love her and her son as they deserved to be loved. Not as much as Wade would love them, but they'd be happy.

"Joubert syndrome is a genetic condition." At her nod acknowledging that she understood this, he added, "I may be a carrier of the gene that causes the disability."

"Then why don't you get tested? With a family history like yours, doctors can screen for that sort of possibility."

There was no anger in her response. Just an overwhelming concern for him. And that concern, that caring, was what made each minute with her more risky. For, the longer he was in her company, the more at risk he was of falling in love with her.

Falling *deeper* in love with her, he thought, berating himself for letting it go this far.

"Not Joubert's. It's so rare that scientists haven't yet isolated the gene that carries it." He took a deep breath and admitted what he'd not dared to speak out loud ever since his brother's birth. "There's a chance a child of mine might be born with disabilities."

She looked away, letting her gaze follow the flight of the small bird that darted from branch to deck rail and finally to the nest in the door wreath.

"I just can't take that chance."

When she returned her pale brown eyes to his, her attitude had hardened. "Life is full of risks. Every parent who's ever awaited the birth of their child knows there's the chance their baby might not be perfect." She swept an arm toward the nest. "It could even happen to those birds. But you know what? They'd feed it anyway. And they'd love it just the same as their other babies. Are you saying you're not even as brave as those little birds?"

"If a child of mine was born with Joubert syndrome, there's a strong chance he would have severe disabilities...most likely worse than Sean's. Possibly even fatal." He picked at a flake of chipped paint on the table. "To answer your question, yes, I'd love the child. And that's exactly why I don't want to bring a kid into the world with so many strikes against him."

He reached for her, touched her shoulder, and willed her to understand that his was not a selfish concern. Rather, it was a selfless one. After all, look at what he was sacrificing—the most beautiful and intriguing woman he'd ever met, not to mention her lovable little boy—to spare a child such a fate.

"That's why I decided early that I would not marry anyone who was still of childbearing age."

Releasing her grip on the table edge, Geneva now crossed her arms over her chest. Her eyes snapped with fire. "I don't believe you, Wade Matteo."

He stood and paced a few steps before turning to her. "I don't lie," he said evenly.

"No one said you were lying." She remained seated. "I just think you're using this genetic condition as an excuse to avoid getting close to a woman." She leaned toward him as if daring him to deny her assertions. "I think you're afraid."

Wade stood stock-still. A mockingbird let loose a string of unconnected phrases stolen from other birds.

"If you weren't afraid of building a permanent relationship with a woman," she said, picking up the empty basket and rising to stand toe to toe with him, "you would acknowledge there is the possibility of adoption."

Geneva held her ground while the seconds ticked away. She wouldn't blame him if he was angry with her. She'd pushed hard, much harder than she had a right to, given the fact that he'd never made any promises to her. He'd never pretended there could be anything between them other than a landlord-tenant relationship, or at most a benign friendship.

But as she'd pointed out, something had passed between them. Something that bound her to him in a way she'd never known with anyone else. And she knew he'd felt it, too. And that it frightened him even more than it did her.

He leveled a gaze at her that swept her soul. "Not for you," he said simply.

She lowered her face, unable to confront his kind and knowing expression. He was the one with the genetic condition, and yet he was offering her his unspoken sympathy. How had things gotten reversed?

Anyone who knew her for more than a day understood that she wanted more children. And she had once revealed to Wade that she'd enjoyed being pregnant and how much she wanted to repeat the experience. Why should it surprise her that he wouldn't want to get involved with her for this very reason?

Geneva didn't doubt that he'd love any child born to him, and accept it no matter what its condition. But she'd come slowly and painfully to the conclusion that he could not love *her*. He could not accept her for who she was…a woman determined to increase her family and the love within it.

But wasn't the same true of her? Hadn't she refused to accept Wade for who he was…a man determined to keep his family as it was? Unchanged and unthreatened?

All along, her head had known that nothing could come of a relationship between them. And now, finally, her heart was in agreement.

Lifting a hand toward her, he cupped her shoulder and held it there for a moment. With a wan smile, he said, "If you want, I can drive by the movie theater later tonight and make sure everything's going okay on your date with Dan."

He was trying to lighten the mood. But what he'd done was gently remind her that she should be directing her affections elsewhere. Just as she had intended to do when she'd accepted the date with Dan.

"No, that won't be necessary," she said, resolution deepening her voice. "I'm sure everything will work out fine between us."

She would see to it that it did.

The wingback chair in the formal living room held a certain amount of sentimental value because his mother had prized it so, but it was not the most comfortable furniture for sitting. The den, which Geneva referred to as the family room, was a much more inviting place for relaxing.

But Wade wasn't relaxing tonight. He was listening for Dan's car to pull into the driveway, bringing Geneva safely home. The movie had ended an hour ago, and dusk was quickly turning to dark. He had no doubts that Dan was a perfect gentleman, but he'd thought she would be back by now.

The room had grown dark, but he didn't bother to switch on the light. Instead, he'd just sit here until he knew she had returned, then leave before she let herself in. There was no sense letting her think he was worrying about her.

He had just decided that if she wasn't home in the next twenty or thirty minutes, he would go out looking for her. Then he heard a car door slam.

Daniel Etheridge came around the car and held the door open for her. He was truly one of the nicest and most charming men Geneva had ever met. As he took her arm in his to escort her up the brick path to the broad front porch of the renovated farmhouse, she ran a mental checklist of his many good qualities.

Dan was smart. He held a well-paying job and was even being groomed by his uncle to take over the family business. He was kind, gentle, patient, strong and healthy...all good traits for a father-to-be. And they shared a number of common interests. Best of all, Dan wanted to get married someday—there was no way they could avoid that subject since Wade had already brought it up—and have a large, loving family.

The man was a perfect match for her. He met all her criteria.

She stepped up onto the porch, avoiding the board that creaked, in case Wade had gone to bed early. Yep, Dan was her dream come true. A bit serious-minded perhaps, but no less wonderful for it.

As they approached the door, he released her arm and turned to face her. Goodness, and he had the classic good looks that no woman could find fault with. He was going to kiss her good-night, and she had no doubt he'd be the perfect gentleman. After all, he was perfect in every other way.

Too bad the spark was missing.

Geneva tilted her head back and waited for the inevitable. Maybe this would help distract her thoughts from the man she'd been trying to forget about all night. When Dan kissed her, it was as perfect as the rest of him. Not too forceful, not too gentle. Just right. And yet still all wrong. Still no spark.

Maybe the problem was with her. Maybe she needed to ignite something between them by starting a kiss that would catch their socks on fire. And burn away all thoughts of Wade.

Geneva threw her arms around Dan's neck and pressed her lips firmly to his. Recalling the kisses that she and Wade had shared, she tried to reenact the experience with a fervor that would have unglued any other mortal man.

Dan seemed momentarily taken aback by her boldness, but willingly accepted her hearty efforts.

Still nothing.

There was no explaining it. They had lots in common. He was a good kisser. And she wanted to be swept off her feet. Perhaps if she deepened the kiss…

"Would you like to sit on the porch swing?"

He nodded and joined her there where they continued their unspoken discussion. Dan held her in his arms—a comfortable place to be—and they kissed again. Perhaps the relaxing sway of the swing would help them find the mutual ground they both sought.

A long moment passed, and eventually it ended without a single firework. Not even a teensy sparkler.

Dan lifted his head. "It's not working for you either, is it?"

"It must be the technique. Maybe if we tried a different—"

"It's no use." He sat back and pushed at the lock of light brown hair that had fallen onto his forehead.

"But we're a perfect match. I won the high-school home ec award and you're an Eagle Scout. We have similar hobbies and interests, we both want a large family, and we're so traditional we could be a 1950s couple," she said, counting off the similarities on her fingers.

"Yeah, but there's one major difference."

"What's that?"

"One of us is in love with Wade."

Geneva's response came so fast and so automatically, it retorted like gunfire. "No!"

He'd heard the car door slam, then footsteps on the porch. That was his cue to retreat to his bedroom. But the bedroom was the last place Wade needed to be when Geneva was on his mind. Which was almost always.

Rising from the too-straight chair, he moved past

the front door and resisted the urge to spy on them through the part in the curtains. But the gesture was less than noble...it would have been too dark to see anything anyway.

That didn't keep him from noticing the squeak of the porch swing as they settled onto it. He tried not to think of what that foretold. His head hoped they were following the scenario in his imagination, but his heart couldn't bear to consider it.

The soft murmur of voices taunted him further, and he hastened to leave the room and go to the far end of the house. But before he reached the hall, he heard Geneva shout a single word. That was all he needed to hear the fear and pain in her voice.

In a smooth motion, he flung open the door, flipped on the light switch and strode out onto the porch to intervene in whatever way was necessary. Best friend or not, Dan would suffer the consequences if he'd done anything to harm Geneva.

Wade came to a sudden halt before them, his fists clenched and teeth gritted.

To his surprise, the other man reacted as if nothing was wrong. In fact, he was laughing. "See?" Dan told Geneva. "Looks like a two-way street, if you ask me."

Geneva merely sat there, her eyes wide but not with fear. Rather, she tilted her head and stared at Wade as if seeing him for the first time...as if she'd come to some earth-shaking realization.

"Geneva?" Suddenly he forgot about Dan. All he could think of was making sure all was well with Geneva. Sinking to one knee beside her, he took her hand in his and patted it to bring her back from her thunderstruck demeanor. "Are you all right?"

She blinked as if clearing the fog from her mind, then smiled at him. A beautiful, glorious smile that made her glow with the radiance of it.

"What is it?" he urged. "What's wrong?"

"I'll tell you what's wrong," Dan said, rising from the swing and pounding him jovially on the back. "You're a blind fool. And a whack matchmaker, to boot."

Chapter Nine

Geneva stepped up onto the sturdy oak coffee table and adjusted the billowing folds of fabric around her legs. The bridesmaid dresses had been a snap, but the bride's gown was quite another matter.

The marbled mirror tiles she'd put on the walls to make the room look larger turned out to have the dual benefit of serving as a dressing mirror. Peering at her all-white reflection, she saw that the bodice puckered at the side darts. And the plain silk taffeta fabric seemed to enhance and even spotlight the faint crinkle.

She had to get this right. This was her first wedding contract with a country-club member—a quite vocal one, Wade had told her when he brought her the job—and the quality of workmanship in these dresses would determine whether she would receive any word-of-mouth referrals for future weddings.

Reaching behind her, she gathered some of the fabric to pull the bodice tighter against her. Although the same height as she, her client was bigger-busted. Perhaps the bride's fuller figure would tighten the seams in the upper part of the dress and cause them to lie flat.

Wade straightened his tie and strode into the den toward the garage. This morning he would be presenting a check to the children's hospital. The charity ball had been a tremendous success, and the check in his breast pocket would go a long way toward the cost of the diagnostic equipment that was needed for the newborn unit. Perhaps, with the aid of state-of-the-art technology, guesswork would be reduced and families would get early and accurate treatment for their children.

Noticing the connecting door to Geneva's place was open, he changed course and moved to close it. She'd been acting rather weird about maintaining their "separateness" lately. It wouldn't be long until the birds flew the nest. Until then, he'd work harder to give her the privacy she craved.

And the distance he needed. He kept reminding himself she was the marrying kind. For all he knew, she might wind up marrying his best friend... assuming, of course, Dan had meant it as a compliment when he'd called him a "whack matchmaker."

He moved to the door to close it, but a glimpse of white caught his eye, and he was immediately mesmerized by the sight. Geneva, standing on the table like a goddess on a pedestal, was wrapped in flowing white. Except for two thin straps, her shoulders were bare, drawing attention to the loose-fitting top that hinted coyly at the treasure hidden within. The rest of the dress eased gently over her hips and flowed down her legs to a small pool of white at her bare feet.

Wade's breath caught in his throat. Guilt stabbed at his conscience for watching her without her knowledge, but he couldn't drag his eyes away from the sight. He was reacting in a way that was totally inappropriate toward the bride-to-be of his best friend. And then it struck him that the white dress she now wore was a wedding gown.

She and Dan couldn't have progressed this far in just a couple of days. Could they? The thought irritated him, and his grip tightened on the door's edge. It moved under the pressure, creaking in protest.

Geneva turned, her hair cascading like a waterfall down her back. "Oh, Wade, it's you."

He frowned. "Were you expecting someone else?"

"Actually, when I heard the noise, I automatically thought it was Jacob." She laughed at the joke she was telling on herself. "I'm so used to having him around that I keep looking for him, even when he's at his play day at church."

With any luck, she'd have a half-dozen children underfoot someday. And all but Jacob would look like Dan. Wade ground his teeth again.

"I'm sorry to have disturbed you." He reached for the door to pull it shut, but she stopped him with the mere whisper of his name.

"Would you do me a favor?" she asked, turning away from him to face the mirror tiles.

He'd give anything she asked for…any but the one thing she needed and wanted most. "Sure."

"Help me smooth out the fabric on this dress."

Reluctantly, Wade crossed the room to her. He

shouldn't be anywhere near her. Every time they got close to each other, his good sense left him and he forgot why they weren't meant to be together.

He'd do it quickly and leave before he had a chance to notice the smoothness of her shoulders or how small and delicate she looked in that dress. Steeling himself, he made a show of looking at his watch and saw that she'd caught the gesture in the mirror. "I have an appointment."

"It'll only take a minute."

She had no idea how right she was. It would only take a minute for him to catch a whiff of her fresh cinnamon scent or take note of the way her tongue darted out as she concentrated on her work. And from there his thoughts would naturally drift to having his lips on hers the next time she swept her tongue across them.

"All I need you to do is hold the fabric and pull it snug between my shoulder blades."

But he would have to touch her.

Geneva turned to offer him her back, reaching behind her head to lift the unrestrained curls so he could more easily grasp the fabric. It was the same pose she might take if they were in a bedroom together, with her waiting for him to undo her dress as they prepared to make love. As he moved toward her, he quickly crossed himself. He needed a power higher than his own to resist her right now. Standing this close to her as he pinched a couple inches of slack material, he imagined he could feel a charge passing between them.

She may have felt it, too. The table wobbled slightly—or did her knees tremble?—and she reached for him, laying a hand on his shoulder to steady herself. Her small hand noticeably shook. All it would have taken to break the sizzling connection between them was to release her gown and step away, but he couldn't bring himself to do it. She was looking at him, her pale pink lips pursed in anticipation of what might happen next. The most logical thing to do right now was to kiss her. After all, she seemed to be expecting something along that line.

Instead, he supported her with a hand to her waist, working hard to ignore the feminine flare of her soft curves. That being impossible, he decided to ease the tension by making light of it.

"Having Cinderella daydreams again?"

Her fingers relaxed against his shoulder, and she blew out a sigh that she'd apparently been suppressing.

"I can't help it that I want a fairy-tale marriage. But it seems that's an unrealistic expectation." Releasing his arm, she touched the spot at the side of her breast where the material had been sewn together. Something on the underside of the garment caused it to stick out slightly.

"These seams refuse to lie flat. I can't expect the bride to wear a flawed dress on the most perfect day of her life."

"Can't you sew them down so they'll stay smooth?"

Geneva turned to face him and gave a patient smile, as if she didn't blame him for not understanding the finer points of her profession. "Unfortunately, that would draw attention to the stitches."

The added height from standing on the table put the offending seams directly at his eye level. But that's not where his gaze went. Drawing his eyes upward to meet hers, he saw the frustration that went beyond the problem with the dress.

"It seems like everything I come into contact with has one big flaw. I move into the perfect place, and almost immediately a couple of birds disrupt my life. I try to find a suitable daddy for Jacob, but one guy doesn't have a sense of humor over a little ice-cream accident, and the other is simply a jerk."

She spread her arms, and Wade took a step back to avoid being accidentally flailed.

"I don't know," she continued with a tone of resignation. "Maybe I have one big flaw in me, too. Perhaps I have a personality defect that I'm not aware of. Or maybe I'm just too blind to see that the perfect man doesn't exist for me."

Wade moved closer and clasped her hands in his. "You're perfect just the way you are," he said with utmost sincerity. "Don't ever change yourself to fit someone else's idea of what you should be. As for the perfect man..." He squeezed her fingers and gave an encouraging smile. "...he's right under your nose."

It practically killed him to push her into the arms of another man, even if it was his best friend. Wade would never be happy about turning away the most wonderful woman ever to step into his life, but if she could be content—happy, even—in a relationship with someone as fine as Dan Etheridge, then he was all for it.

"When Jacob is tired or upset or just needs a hug, you identify the problem and do whatever's needed, right?"

At her nod, he hammered in the nails that would

seal the coffin on whatever might have come between them.

"And you're not the kind of woman to sit back and wait passively for Prince Charming to sweep you off your feet. If there's a fixable problem, you need to identify it so you can go after what you want." If there was something that Geneva saw as a flaw in Dan, then he was certain it was minor. "Don't let a small problem keep you from pursuing a lifetime of happiness with the man who's right for you." He looked up at her, beseeching her with his eyes to do the right thing and allow a relationship with Dan to grow. "Love is too important to throw away over what might be one clump of crabgrass on an otherwise well-tended green."

Geneva drew in a sharp breath. Had she heard him correctly? Was he telling her not to give up on him? Recalling the previous night, she thought of what Dan had said...that Wade's protective behavior proved he loved her in return.

The man standing before her, his head tilted upward in silent expectation, was a proud man, one who had worked hard to build up his defenses and was now asking for her help in breaking them down. Although he was not in the classic bended-knee position, his posture was that of a man preparing to pop an all-important question.

"It's something both people have to work at. Both people have to give a little so they can meet in the middle." Once again capturing her hand, he brought it to his chest, where she could feel the beat of his heart. After a moment, he lifted her hand and held it out between them for a long moment...so long that she thought he might kiss her fingers. But he merely held it there, a visual example of two people meeting in the middle. "Perhaps you need to make the first move toward that common ground. Are you willing to do that?"

Going against the little voice that had sent her repeated warnings ever since she'd met Wade, Geneva responded with a mute nod. What did that little voice know, anyway? If two people loved each other and were committed to overcoming the minor obstacles standing between them, then a relationship could certainly work.

Every time Jacob returned home from an outing, even before playing, eating or retrieving his favorite action figure from the place of honor on his dresser, he always sought out their landlord. And as her son toddled through the house calling Wade's name, Geneva often found herself hoping just as strongly that Wade was home and would spring out from behind a door or the convenient hiding spot beside the refrigerator to scoop him up in his arms in a joyous celebration of homecoming. And just as often as that happened, Geneva secretly wished it was she whom Wade twirled with dizzying glee about the room.

"You're right. I'll have to make the first move," she said at last. Then, staring directly into his emerald eyes, she asked him the question that would confirm or break her decision. "Will you help me?"

"Of course," he said without hesitation. "I'm here for you."

That was all she needed. A promise that he would meet her halfway. She moved to step down from the table, and Wade again touched a strong hand to her waist. Someday, if things went as she wished, he would hold her waist much like this on their wedding night, pulling her to him so they could meet in the middle…on the common ground of their love and mutual attraction. "I just hope I'll handle it the right way."

"You will," he said, releasing her as her feet hit the floor. "You have my vote of confidence. I'm sure you won't let me down."

She stood before him, wishing she had the nerve to take the first move right now and seal their new-found accord with a kiss. But his stance was uninviting, which seemed surprising after their heart-to-heart agreement to pursue a relationship together.

Silence filled the awkward gap between them, broadening the unexpected chasm until she was prompted to fill it with words…safe words. Words that would move the subject away from how they might find that common ground to something she felt only slightly more confident about tackling.

"I wish it could be as easy to fix this gown. Maybe I should just throw it out and start over."

"There's no reason to trash a perfectly good dress. Just make the stitches something people will want to look at."

That said, he picked up an embroidered pillow from the sofa, tossed it to her and moved to the door.

Hugging it to her, she crossed the room and watched as he went into his den and picked up his briefcase. He was taking the proceeds from the charity ball to the children's hospital. When Cherise and Renee had warned her Wade was only after one thing, they'd been referring to donations to his favorite cause…research and diagnostic equipment for children born with birth defects. Yes, he had charmed many of the influential women in Kinnon Falls and sold himself at bachelor auctions, but none of it was done for his own personal gain. It had all been for children…children like his brother who had been unfortunate enough to inherit the wrong genes from their parents.

Despite their surface differences, she and Wade were very much alike in the ways that counted.

After all the headway they'd made, he was leaving? Just like that? He'd offered her an opportunity to salvage things between them—to start a relationship despite his concern about fathering a child with Joubert syndrome—and now he was walking away as if they'd just put their relationship on hold?

Maybe it was a test. Maybe he was trying to force her into making that first move now. Force her to decide if a union with him was worth fighting for.

It was. His medical situation was that solitary bit of crabgrass on an entire eighteen-hole green. And it was up to her to deal with it. Now was as good a time as any.

She returned the pillow to the sofa and followed him into the den where he was double-checking the contents of his briefcase before leaving for his appointment. Geneva cleared her throat. When he looked up, fixing those incredible green eyes on her, she summoned the courage to speak directly about the subject that had previously been denied by both of them.

"You once told me you couldn't love me the way I needed to be loved." It felt awkward to say the words out loud, especially since she'd assumed the fault lay with her expectations for a permanent love and forever kind of commitment…expectations that many people saw as quaint, naive and even old-fashioned in this day and age. "But you were wrong."

He closed the briefcase and straightened.

"When you rushed out onto the porch after my date with Dan, well, I knew then—"

"I've always been very protective of others." He jerked away from her, as if dismissing the notion of what she'd been about to say. "Too protective, maybe. Just ask Sean."

"The feelings that prompted you to intervene had nothing to do with a sibling kind of love or even neighborly concern. The feelings we have for each other, that's the way I need to be loved."

He shook his head. His fingers tightened on the briefcase handle. "You know that's not what I meant."

"It doesn't matter," she said, taking a step toward him, closer to the middle ground they both sought. In response, he took a step closer to the exit. "You yourself said we're the perfect couple. That one small problem, like your genetic condition, is something we can overcome if we're willing to make sacrifices."

Wade put down the briefcase and rubbed a hand across his clenched jaw. When he spoke, he didn't meet her gaze. "I was talking about you and Dan. He can be a little inflexible at times, but if you are willing to meet each other in the middle, you two will be the perfect match." This time he met her eyes. "I've never seen two people better suited for each other."

Geneva felt a chill pass over her as the impact of his words hit her square in the heart. He hadn't been encouraging her to take a chance on loving him, on overcoming the one obstacle that stood in the path of their everlasting happiness. No, he'd merely been pushing her away again, into the arms of another man.

Geneva sucked in her breath, nearly filling out the flawed bodice. None of that mattered, though. She had seen the look in his eyes when he'd burst onto the porch like a white knight on a stallion, determined to rescue the damsel he loved. He had teased her about her fairy-tale dreams, not recognizing that he was the living, breathing embodiment of all that she wished for. And, like any worthy princess, she would not let this noble knight get away without standing up to the two dragons that threatened to devour them…one being the problem of how children could or would fit into their relationship, and the other being Wade's dogged stubbornness.

"Dan is a fine person," she said, "but I don't want him. I want *you.*"

Abandoning the reticence he'd shown earlier, Wade came to her and gently gripped her arms. "You also want babies."

In the overall scheme of things, his unwillingness to play roulette with genetic probabilities was, as he had put it, crabgrass on the course to happiness for the two of them. For the *three* of them, for Jacob loved Wade, too. As he had suggested, she would break their impasse by making the first move in coming toward a common meeting ground.

"I want you more than I want babies."

The green in his eyes darkened to that of a winter pine on a cloud-filled day. It was obvious he knew what she was suggesting, what she was prepared to sacrifice to make things work between them, and he didn't seem at all happy with her decision.

He released her and jammed his hands into his

pockets. The gesture signaled a retreat, not only from her physically, but of the heart as well.

"We've been over this before." And it was clear from the way he looked at her that he had not changed his mind since their earlier discussion. "You have the nesting instinct, and you'll never be completely happy until your home is overflowing with adorable little babies who have your taffy-colored eyes and curly brown hair."

Wade watched as she dropped her chin and began smoothing imaginary wrinkles from the white dress. He knew without her saying it that she could not argue with the truth he'd just spoken.

Worse, he knew he had hurt Geneva yet again. Although he doubted he'd ever felt worse in his life, he knew it was for the best. For all of them.

He picked up his briefcase and moved toward the utility room, refusing to see the raw, open pain in her eyes. He stood in the doorway a moment, dredging up the strength to deliver yet another volley...one that would leave no question as to where they stood with each other.

"It would be best," he said, pausing until he had her full attention, "if we go back to thinking of our relationship as the business arrangement it was meant to be."

"Don't forget to brown the beef before you put it in the pot."

Sean pressed his hands together in what Geneva had come to learn was his gesture of impatience. "I know," he said, pointing to the open book on the table. "That's what it says in the recipe."

She smiled her apology. Of course he had things

under control. In her eagerness to help, she'd failed to recognize that he hadn't yet started the beef browning because he was still slowly and methodically placing potatoes in the automatic peeler gadget. The simple task would take forever at the rate he was going. She had to let him move at his own pace, which seemed to be stuck in the slow position, but that didn't mean she couldn't give him a hand with what was left.

"Next time you make soup," she said, picking up a potato and paring knife, "be sure to give yourself extra preparation time."

Sean flashed her a charming grin that reminded her of a certain other Matteo male. "Why? I'm in no rush."

She pursed her lips and met his twinkling gaze. Not quite twenty, he was unaware of the importance mothers place on getting their youngsters fed on a regular schedule. As if he knew she was thinking of him, Jacob let out a squeal as his toy car took a sharp turn around the table leg where he played.

"Do you think this will be enough for all four of us?" Sean waved a hand toward the pot where the carrots and onions awaited the potatoes.

His invitation for all of them to have dinner together meant breaking Wade's edict that they maintain a purely business relationship between them, but she didn't have the heart to refuse her young neighbor's generous offer. He had quite a flair for cooking, and she wanted to encourage his new interest and independence.

"Sure. Jacob won't eat much. In fact, you might want to fix almost this much even when you're cooking just for yourself. Soup makes great leftovers."

Sean finished peeling his potato and wordlessly

took the one from her hand, his knowing expression all the reproach she needed to back off and let him prepare the dinner himself. He didn't want or need her help peeling the potatoes, so she resigned herself to helping with the ongoing cleanup that went with the job of cooking.

Retrieving a section of the morning's paper, she unfolded it and began piling the peels onto the pages. As she did so, a photo leaped out at her from the society page. Folding the page back over the brown strips, Geneva groaned at what she saw.

There on page B6 of the Kinnon Falls *Register*— in full color, no less—was a four-column shot of her and Wade. Sure, there were other people in the background, mostly local notables whose names often appeared in print, but it was she and Wade who danced together in the foreground, drawing attention to the sizzling interplay going on between them. And if that publicly displayed moment didn't make her cringe, the caption sure did.

Country-club owner Wade Matteo cuts the rug with new lady-love Geneva Johnson. His live-in friend has prompted worried bachelorettes to speculate whether this is the one who'll finally clip this playboy's wings, or if she's just the latest source of his legendary freewheeling entertainment. Entertainment was the key word for the evening when Mayor Fishbein later grabbed the microphone and belted out a tune....

The article that accompanied the photo went on to explain that the proceeds from the fund-raiser would go toward the purchase of a new MRI machine.

Geneva sank into the chair opposite Sean as the full impact of the photograph and teaser lines hit her. She could see how easy it would be to interpret the smoldering exchange between the couple in the picture as evidence of a burgeoning romance. But the disclaimer that followed the supposition—the more predictable possibility that Wade had merely found a new play toy—put all such notions of romance and commitment back into perspective. Everyone knew that the likelihood of the town's playboy settling down with one woman was far-fetched.

Instead, she'd been referred to as his "live-in friend," which was exactly the kind of notoriety she'd feared would come with being seen in the company of Wade Matteo. For that reason, she was glad they'd misspelled Jensen. But with an unusual first name like Geneva—not to mention a clear shot of her face— she doubted she'd be able to slip back into the safety of obscurity anytime soon.

Worse than the smear on her reputation was the knowledge that she'd been unwittingly plunged into a perpetual purgatory of singlehood. Although she would gladly "clip his wings," if only she knew how, Wade had made it painfully clear that he would not give up his freedom to her or any woman for another ten years or more.

Even if she had wanted to move on and start over with someone else right away, who would have her after this? But she didn't want anyone else. She wanted Wade, the one man she loved like no other. And he was denying her—denying them both—a chance for the kind of happiness that could fill an eternity.

Geneva's face and neck burned hot, and a lump formed deep in her throat.

Jacob looked up at her from where he sat playing on the floor. "Watch dis," he said, and proceeded to "wreck" the plastic race car.

Geneva stiffened her resolve and gave him a brave smile. Content that he'd had her full attention for that brief moment, he went back to running the vehicle along the lines on the tiled floor.

While her son was occupied, she sought to busy herself cleaning up the potato, onion and carrot scraps. She would not let herself cry over a man again, especially one she'd known from the start was intent on maintaining his bachelor status. Especially not the one who, if circumstances had been different, could challenge her, excite her and satisfy her like no other.

The memory of some of the sweet things he'd done for her bubbled up from the recesses of her mind. Giving her his house key to avoid displacing a family of birds. Comforting her with hugs and tender kisses after she thought Jacob had wandered outside and gotten lost. Rescuing her from the obnoxious doctor. Giving her the job of designing and sewing new uniforms for his staff and referring new clients to her. Those memories threatened to overwhelm her, threatened to fill her eyes with more than the misting the onions had caused.

Wrapping the newspaper photo around the compost material, she got up to throw it out. The vegetable scraps and any chance of a relationship with Wade would go on the trash heap.

Sean put down the potato and stilled her jerky

movements with a hand to her wrist. "You don't have to baby-sit me," he said in his slow, halting voice. "I'll call you when dinner is ready."

Geneva considered the meaning behind his words as she went outside with the paper wad. Not only had Wade been overprotective in arranging with her to keep a watchful eye on Sean, he'd also underestimated his younger brother's ability to lead a productive life. It helped that they lived so close together and that Wade was able to provide him with a job he enjoyed, but a hired watchdog was not necessary.

Sean was right, he didn't want a baby-sitter. What he wanted was his independence. Not in quite the same way that his older brother wanted his freedom, but she was prepared to give them both what they sought. Opening the trash-can lid, she took one last look at the smiling couple in the newspaper and made her decision. The bundle fell into the can with a solid thud.

Going back into Sean's kitchen, she called to Jacob to pick up his toys. Then, with forced cheeriness, she told their dinner host, "We're going to go back to our place now and leave you to do your own thing. I'm sure the soup will be delicious."

He smiled and picked up the last unpeeled potato as she moved toward the door that would take them through Wade's house to their own apartment. Their landlord would dine with them tonight. But despite the possible awkwardness of the situation, she couldn't have said no to her young friend's invitation. Rather, she would celebrate Sean's accomplishment, knowing this would be her last meal with either of the brothers.

As she stepped over the threshold into the main part of the house, she collided with Wade, clutched his arms for balance and they both spun twice around the other before coming to a stop. Although Geneva knew better, she attributed her dizzy breathlessness to the balancing act they'd just performed.

"Wade's funny," said the tiny commentator from behind her.

Wade bent over and gave the little guy a fake punch to the gut. "Something smells good."

He was looking at her as he said it, making Geneva wonder if he was talking about her. Since Sean hadn't yet cooked the beef, started the vegetables simmering or added spices to the soup, it wasn't likely Wade was talking about their dinner. Unless, of course, he was referring to the raw, diced onions his brother had shed tears over, which was doubtful. Nevertheless, she intentionally misunderstood his remark.

"Vegetable beef soup," she said in an ever-so-businesslike manner. "Sean will call us when it's ready."

Drawing a hand across his evening-shadowed jaw, he asked, "Aren't you going to stay and supervise until it's done?"

Geneva reached for Jacob's hand, knowing the contact would bolster her resolve in the decision she'd made. Knowing it would be better for both her and her son to make a fresh start before they became too entrenched in their current surroundings...and before the two men in this house worked their way deeper into their hearts.

"Sean doesn't need me," she said, hoping Wade would understand that she wasn't just referring to tonight, but in general.

When he started to protest, she cut him off with a resigned shake of her head.

"The same goes for you." Then she delivered her final salvo. "We can't live here anymore."

Chapter Ten

Wade leaned back on his elbows and braced himself as Jacob ran to him and launched his tiny body at his midsection. Even though he'd tightened his muscles, the little dynamo knocked the wind out of him.

Wade fell back on the grass and held his hands in a time-out signal while he recovered from the horse-play and laughter. Jacob followed in kind, aping his actions.

When Wade could breathe normally again, he sat up and eyed the little boy who'd kept him going at top speed for the past hour and a half while Geneva scouted for a new place to live. He understood her desire to break their ties now, before they started to feel like a permanent part of each other's lives. He only wished, well, he shouldn't be thinking about his wishes. He should be concerned about what was best for Jacob. And Geneva.

"Do it again," Jacob said, jumping to his feet with

that perpetual-motion kind of energy that he applied to everything he did.

"No, that's enough for now." Geneva had warned him not to get the kid too stirred up or Jacob would never be able to wind down enough to take an afternoon nap. So Wade distracted him with something a little less boisterous. "Watch this."

He plucked a blade of grass, lifted it to his mouth and blew. The shrieking sound caused Jacob to press his hands over his ears. But that lasted only a second. In the next instant, the boy yanked up a stalk of grass, roots and all, and puffed ineffectually at it.

"Here, try it this way." Wade demonstrated by eliciting another shriek from their makeshift musical instrument, then leaned toward the boy, stretching the blade between his thumbs. This time when Jacob tried it, the result was a high-pitched squeak. A grin plumped his cheeks before he grabbed the grass from Wade's fingers and toddled away.

"Hey, where are you going?"

"Gonna show Uncle Sean."

The innocent pronouncement knocked Wade harder than the thirty-pound boy landing full-force on his stomach. Maneuvering past Jacob, he halted the boy's progress by kneeling in front of him. "Who told you to call him that?"

"Uncle Sean." After his matter-of-fact reply, he darted past Wade and hurled himself toward the subject of their discussion, who had just stepped out onto his stoop. As if understanding that he couldn't fire himself into Sean's legs the way he often did with Wade, Jacob slowed at the last possible moment and greeted him with a hug instead.

Sean returned the gesture of affection and then

asked, as if he hadn't already guessed the answer, "What's all the racket out here?"

"My whistle." Jacob opened his fist and displayed the crumpled bit of grass.

The two pals spent the next couple of moments discussing which was louder, the grass whistle or the teapot. Then Jacob urged him over to the ground-level deck to inspect a caterpillar he'd found earlier.

Wade watched the pair, knowing it would be difficult for all of them, including Sean, when Geneva and Jacob moved away. The mother and son had only been in their lives less than a month, but they already felt like members of the family, as evidenced by Sean's adding the title of "Uncle" to his name.

As Sean's crutch thumped against the wooden planks of the deck, the baby birds mistook the vibration for their parents' return. The little brood clung precariously to the edge of the nest, each peeping insistently that it should be the first one fed.

Alerted by the miniature chorus, Jacob tugged at Sean's shorts. "Let me see!"

His brother cast the boy a look that showed he was torn between what his heart and mind wanted to do and what his body could deliver. He lifted one crutch in silent explanation.

That was when Wade intervened. "Jacob, my boy, you can't ask Sean to put down his magic swords," he said, closing the distance between them and scooping him up. "The evil troll might steal them when he's not looking!"

Jacob giggled, but seemed enthralled by the make-believe excuse. Before the kid could demand his own pair of magic swords, Wade turned him so he could see into the crowded nest.

"The babies are getting bigger now. We have to be very quiet," he warned, "so we don't scare them into flying away before their muscles are strong enough."

"When Uncle Sean's muscles gets big..." Jacob held up a scrawny arm and flexed like his favorite wrestling hero on television. "...he's gon' fly."

Wade caught his brother's amused grin and tried not to laugh at Jacob's serious declaration. It was apparent he had taken Geneva's explanation that Sean's muscles were weak and given it his own spin. "Don't bet the farm on it."

"I don't gots a farm."

The boy seemed truly puzzled, so Wade figured he'd better come up with a more proper response. Shifting him to his other arm, he pointed to the birds who'd given up hope of a fresh morsel and closed their beaks. They stared back with shiny, unblinking black eyes.

"The birds have feathers that help them fly," he explained. "But people don't have feathers, so they can't fly."

"Not even Uncle Sean?"

"Not even Sean."

His brother, who stood beside them, cracked up at that last bit. Yep, they sure were going to miss this little guy.

After Sean had recovered from his spell of stifled laughter, he nudged Wade aside to get a closer look. "What's wrong with that one?"

Wade leaned toward the sight. "The big one?"

"Yeah, it looks different than the rest."

Although they were similar in color, shape and

head and belly markings, one nestling's wings and tail had a mottled pattern whereas its siblings' were plain.

Jacob gave his opinion. "It's a evil twoll."

"No, I think it's a house wren in a titmouse's nest. This nest must have been claimed by two sets of birds, with both laying eggs in it before the current parents finally took control."

"Cool," said Sean. "The wren is adopted."

Jacob placed his hand on Wade's chin and tugged gently until he had his full attention. Apparently unable to articulate the question that was on his mind, he merely said, "Huh?"

"Adopted." Wade repeated the word, then realized the boy was probably too young to understand the concept. "That one," he said, gesturing toward the bird they'd been discussing, "is not their baby. He was left there by mistake."

The boy's lower lip came out, and his eyebrows formed peaks of empathy. Wade realized he'd better clarify the situation before tears fell.

"But the new mom and dad love him anyway," he hastily added. "They don't even know he came from somewhere else."

Jacob seemed happy with that explanation. When one of the parent birds chirped angrily at them from the dogwood tree, Wade and Sean stepped away and watched as it entered the nest and began feeding, starting with their adopted chick.

Jacob's attention already wandering, he wiggled to be let down. Wade laughed that the tyke's feet seemed to be spinning before they even touched the ground.

If his life circumstances had been different, Wade would have wanted a kid exactly like Jacob. The boy was a real kick, and it was going to be incredibly quiet around here after he was gone.

Wade tried to picture what it had been like before Jacob and his mother had arrived and was surprised to find that his memory failed him. Intellectually he knew he had gone to work every day, pushed to raise money for the children's hospital and dated various women while still keeping them at arm's length, but he couldn't remember what it had *felt* like to be on his own...with no ties and no desire to settle down with any woman. All he knew was that it felt a hell of a lot better after Geneva had come into his life. It was as if the mother and son had always been here. He knew without a doubt they would always be in his heart, if not in his house.

Then, with a certainty that was as solid as the tricycle Jacob pedaled across the deck, a gut-level impulse told Wade he could not let them go. He loved this child as much as if they were related by blood. He loved him the way those birds loved their foundling baby...only much, much more.

In pursuit of a small blue butterfly, Jacob took a sharp left turn, threatening to overturn the tricycle he rode. Wade shot toward the boy, arms outstretched to prevent a fall, but the kid's well-placed sneaker righted him and he sped away, unconcerned about the near mishap.

Wade's shoulders slumped, and he sat on the edge of the picnic table where he and Geneva had shared those terrific kisses. Sean was right. He was overprotective. Not only had he underestimated his brother's abilities, he'd also underestimated Geneva's ability to love. He'd made assumptions about her very natural desire for children, and then tried to protect her from the pain he'd mistakenly thought she'd suffer if she did not give birth to her own brood.

He hadn't given Geneva the credit she deserved. If a feathered mom could love another baby as her own, then certainly Geneva could do that and more. With sudden clarity, Wade knew that she would willingly and lovingly accept an adopted child into her family. He'd been incredibly unfair to her.

"I am so stupid," he said, hitting the heel of his hand against his forehead.

Sean cracked a teasing grin. "Yeah, I know, but I love you anyway, brother." Using one crutch to wave a goodbye salute to Jacob, he turned toward his golf cart. "Gotta get back to work. See you later, Geneva."

Wade started at the mention of her name. Lost deep in thought, he hadn't even heard her return.

Squealing his delight, Jacob threw himself at her, and Wade fought the desire to do the same.

Geneva gave Jacob a hug. Their welcome-home ritual accomplished, he tottered off to play in the sandbox. She pushed her hair behind her shoulder, then nervously clutched the document that would bring an end to the recent developments in her life. To the hopes she'd fostered and the dreams she'd built. And to the love that had grown between her and Wade.

No, that was wrong. Nothing would ever end her love for Wade. But maybe, with time, she'd be able to put the pain aside and move on. She'd have to move on...for Jacob's sake, if not her own.

Wade rose from the picnic table and approached her, standing closer than most landlords and tenants would feel comfortable doing. His gaze bored into her, his focus seeringly intense. If Geneva had had

the willpower, she would have stepped away to break
the powerful grip that seemed to hold them together.
But she didn't move, preferring to take in the unique
currents that surged between them, imprinting them
on her brain, her body, her soul, knowing that the
memory of him would be all she'd have after her
plans were set in motion.

"Did you find a new place?"

She nodded and lifted the sheet of rolled paper.
"The place is mine after I sign the lease. I can move
in this weekend."

"So soon."

A cloud shadowed his face, and Geneva wondered
if he was upset that he would have no one to watch
after Sean.

"Your brother will be fine," she assured him.
"I've been checking around, and there's a service in
Kinnon Falls for people with disabilities. The agency
offers life-skills training, physical therapy and a
chance to meet people who are faced with similar
challenges."

Wade's only response was to nod solemnly.

Still unwilling to break eye contact, she merely
said, "I'll go start packing." She and Jacob had their
welcome-home ritual. What kind of ritual did one do
to mark the end of what could have been a wonderful
relationship?

"Before you do that, I need your help." His expression had softened, and it seemed important that
she oblige his request. "We have to dig a hole."

Jacob grabbed his plastic shovel from the sandbox
and ran toward them. "I help!"

"Of course you will," Wade said, scooping the

boy up in his arms. "Because you're part of the reason I need to bury something."

Jacob bounced delightedly in his arms and swung his shovel. Wade set him to work at a patch of ground off the edge of the deck and turned back to Geneva.

Reaching for his collar, he removed the Bachelor of the Year pin that had been his daily reminder to play it safe, to avoid commitment at all cost. He handed Geneva the pin. "I don't want that kind of lifestyle anymore," he told her.

She turned the gold pin over in her palm. The lettering had been worn almost smooth and the enamel had thinned under so much handling over the years. "But your freedom…"

He covered her hand with his own. "My freedom is not worth the price I'd pay for it." He squeezed her fingers. "The cost is much too great."

Geneva thought she understood what he was saying, but she feared she may have been reading too much into the gesture. Reluctant to torture her heart with false hopes, she dared not believe that his decision had anything to do with her. She waited pensively for the rest of his explanation.

Opening her fingers, he retrieved the pin. "While we're burying stuff, what do you say we put that lease in there, too?"

With his hand outstretched, he waited for her to give him the sheet of paper she'd been wadding into a wrinkled mess.

Geneva paused, looking away from the deep green of his eyes to the white scrap of paper that represented a life apart from the man she loved…from the man who loved her enough to sacrifice his freedom and commit his heart to her. She had no doubt he'd be as faithful to her as he had been for all those years to his promise not to encumber a woman with his genetic problem.

He was waiting for the paper, waiting for her to give herself symbolically to him as she buried her lease and the choice of a life without him. But she couldn't give it to him. Not just yet. Not until she knew for sure....

"But what about the Joubert syndrome?"

It wasn't an issue that would go away if ignored. If he wanted to hold their family to three—the two of them and Jacob—that would be plenty for her. Being with them was all she needed to be happier than she'd ever been before. But they had to come to an agreement, to know what to expect in the matter of family size, before they took things to the next step.

"It's still a possibility, and I won't know for sure whether I'm a carrier until researchers find out which gene causes the syndrome." He clenched the pin in his fist. "That could be only months away, or it could be years from now."

Slipping the pin into his pocket, he reached out and stroked her cheek, the touch both tentative and hopeful. Geneva turned toward his gentle fingers, her lip brushing his skin.

"If you're willing to wait until then to give birth to my baby, I'd be honored to make you my wife." He lifted her left hand and placed an imaginary ring on her finger. "In the meantime, we'll adopt as many kids as you want. There are a lot of rooms in this house that we can fill."

Stunned, Geneva tried to gather her whirling thoughts and emotions. This was all she had hoped for, and more, but she couldn't help thinking his change of heart was too good to be true. "Are you sure? You said my nesting instinct—"

"I was wrong. It was my attitude, not my genetics or your love of children, that kept us apart." He cleared his throat and began again. "I had no right making that decision for you. If you can forgive me for being such a stubborn fool, let me know by saying yes...that you'll marry me."

Jacob patted her leg with his shovel. "It's a *big* hole!"

Wade grinned at her, and they followed the boy to the inch-deep "crater" he'd dug. As they knelt around it, examining the handiwork, Wade cast Geneva a questioning glance. She hadn't given him his answer, and he was still waiting.

Wordlessly, she squeezed the lease until it was the size of a golf ball, and handed it to him. A broad smile covered her face as her soul filled with happiness at the thought of spending the rest of her life with this wonderful man. He returned her sentiment with a beaming smile of his own.

"This is a terrific hole," Wade told his future son, "but we have to go a bit deeper to hit China." Lifting his gaze to Geneva, he added, "This stuff has to stay down there forever...which is almost as long as I'll be loving you both."

Epilogue

The "aisle" Geneva was set to walk down was nothing more than a white runner between two groups of chairs in the backyard. From her position near the chinaberry tree, newly planted over the bachelor pin and lease, she would walk with Wade to the lake's edge where the minister awaited them. But first she had to get her mother calmed and seated.

"Mom, it's almost time."

"Yes, it is, and nothing is as it should be." The widow snapped the clasp on her purse as if to emphasize her point. "This whole thing is so untraditional."

Geneva touched her mother's arm. "Daddy's not here to walk me down the aisle, so it made sense that Wade and I would walk together."

The older woman said nothing, but set herself to brushing invisible lint from Geneva's white, knee-length dress. She stopped with a sigh as she took in the colorful embroidered bodice.

The white-on-white technique Wade had suggested for her client's gown had looked so good that Geneva had decided to incorporate it into her own design. But she'd used green thread—Jacob's favorite color and the same hue as Wade's eyes—since she felt odd about wearing all white.

"You told Sean not to give Jacob any more candy, didn't you?"

"Yes, Mom. He's safe inside under Aunt Helen's watchful eye."

"Where's your bouquet?"

If she didn't get her mother seated, this wedding would never start. "Don't worry about it. I'll—"

But it was too late. Her mother had already dashed into the house. The bridesmaids clustered at the deck, and best-man Sean chatted with the minister in their positions by the lake.

Geneva felt someone slip his arm around her waist and turned to find Kinnon Falls's most eligible husband-to-be smiling down at her.

"Let's hurry up and do this before you change your mind."

She basked in the glow of his open adoration. "No chance of that. But it wouldn't hurt to get it done before Jacob's naptime."

He winked at her. "I wouldn't mind taking a nap after this is over…as long as it's with you."

Geneva warmed as she considered his suggestion. Luxuriating in his arms was only one of the many reasons she wanted to hurry and get the ceremony over with. Because the sooner they said "I do," the sooner they'd be able to start their life of bliss together.

Her mother returned clutching the bouquet in one

hand and Jacob in the other. Geneva couldn't help admiring how handsome her little boy looked in the suit she'd made for him. To avoid carrying the ring bearer's pillow with its symbolic ring stitched to the center, the clever child had tucked the pillow under his suspender straps. He looked like Santa Claus with a belly ring.

She handed Geneva the bouquet. ''Be sure to turn it so the bird's nest shows among the flowers.''

Geneva did as she was instructed and gave her mother a kiss who, in turn, kissed the groom and ring bearer and scurried down the aisle to her seat. And it was just in time, too. Mere seconds later, the musician sat down at the piano that had been moved from the clubhouse and began playing ''Wind Beneath My Wings,'' the cue for the bridesmaids to lead the way.

As planned, Wade tucked her hand in the crook of his arm, and they proceeded to walk down the aisle together, with Jacob marching slightly ahead. But the toddler had other ideas. Removing the pillow from his suspenders, he laid it on the runner, then got down and placed his head on it, pretending to sleep.

Giggles rippled among the guests, but laughter erupted when the little show-off produced a fake snore.

With an amused grin, her betrothed picked the boy up and carried him as they walked toward the minister to become the family they were meant to be.

As they approached the lakefront ''altar,'' one of the ushers—Tim, the golf pro—stepped away from Sean and raised a seven-iron. Wade's brother grinned at this unrehearsed gesture and lifted a crutch to form the other half of the arch.

Wade paused only an instant, just long enough to

shoot his friend and brother a tolerant grin. He ducked slightly and prompted Geneva to step under it with him. They were met by dueling camera flashes…one from the wedding photographer and the other a newspaper cameraman.

Geneva didn't mind the uninvited man's appearance, though. Let him show the world—or at least all of Kinnon Falls—that she was not Wade's latest plaything…and that her new husband would now be the town's *least* eligible man.

As they came to a halt in front of the preacher, she whispered, "Mom was right. This isn't exactly traditional."

Wade shifted Jacob's weight and lifted her hand to his lips, kissing it tenderly. "Neither am I, but that didn't stop you."

She thought about the more traditional men who, at the time, had seemed like perfect prospects for the altar. A Sunday-school teacher, a doctor and a corporate executive. All very traditional, and all very wrong for her and Jacob.

Geneva smiled up at her soon-to-be husband. There was no question that Wade's love for her was untraditionally strong or that he'd make an untraditionally great dad.

"I'm glad it didn't stop me," she said. "*Very* glad."

And then—breaking tradition yet again—they kissed before the vows were said.

*   *   *   *   *

Don't miss the reprisal of
Silhouette Romance's popular miniseries

**When
King Michael of
Edenbourg goes
missing,**

Royally Wed
The Stanbury Crown

**his devoted
family and loyal
subjects make it
their mission to bring
him home safely!**

Their search begins March 2001 and continues through June 2001.

On sale March 2001: **THE EXPECTANT PRINCESS**
by bestselling author **Stella Bagwell** (SR #1504)

On sale April 2001: **THE BLACKSHEEP PRINCE'S BRIDE**
by rising star **Martha Shields** (SR #1510)

On sale May 2001: **CODE NAME: PRINCE**
by popular author **Valerie Parv** (SR #1516)

On sale June 2001: **AN OFFICER AND A PRINCESS**
by award-winning author **Carla Cassidy** (SR #1522)

Available at your favorite retail outlet.

Where love comes alive™

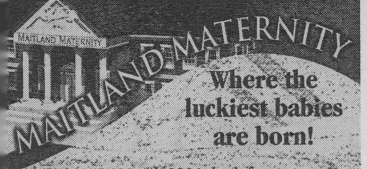

MAITLAND MATERNITY

Where the
luckiest babies
are born!

In March 2001, look for

BILLION DOLLAR BRIDE

by Muriel Jensen

**Billionaire Austin Cahill doesn't believe
in love or marriage—**

he only wants to marry in order to produce an heir. Single
mom and wedding planner Anna Maitland is horrified by his
old-fashioned attitude. So when Austin proposes a marriage
of convenience, will Anna be able to refuse him...
now that she's fallen in love with him?

*Each book tells a different story about the
world-renowned Maitland Maternity Clinic—
where romances are born, secrets are revealed...
and bundles of joy are delivered.*

HARLEQUIN®
Makes any time special™

Silhouette®
Where love comes alive™

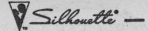

REGENCY ROMANCE

Visit the elegant English countryside, explore the whirlwind of London Society and meet feisty heroines who tame roguish heroes with their wit, zest and feminine charm, in...The Regency Collection.

Available in March 2001 at your favorite retail outlet:

TRUE COLOURS
by Nicola Cornick

THE WOLFE'S MATE
by Paula Marshall

MR. TRELAWNEY'S
PROPOSAL
by Mary Brendan

TALLIE'S KNIGHT
by Anne Gracie